Roger Ormerod lives in Wolverhampton, England, and is the author of more than thirty novels of suspense. He entered the Civil Service in 1937, serving ten years in the county courts. He has also worked as a Social Security inspector, postman and production control officer in a heavy industry factory. In recent years, he has devoted himself to his flourishing career as a novelist, and to his photography and painting.

FINAL TOLL

Johnny Parfitt used to be a driver — until Den talked him into stealing a wagon load of scotch. The plan went disastrously wrong and Johnny was caught, leaving Den free to move in with Johnny's wife. So, on the day he is released from prison, Johnny steals a lorry and heads for Den. But a narrow suspension bridge buckles under the weight of the truck and he is trapped, hanging in mid-air between two cliffs, buffeted by a raging storm. Engineer Colin Marson is called in to direct an impossible rescue — to get Johnny out before the bridge plummets into the swelling river. . .

Books by Roger Ormerod
Published by The House of Ulverscroft:

ROGER ORMEROD

FINAL TOLL

Complete and Unabridged

ULVERSCROFT
Leicester

First published in Great Britain in 1999 by
Severn House Publishers Limited
Surrey

First Large Print Edition
published 2000
by arrangement with
Severn House Publishers Limited
Surrey

F
1379702

British Library CIP Data

Ormerod, Roger, *1920* –
    Final toll.—Large print ed.—
    Ulverscroft large print series: adventure & suspense
    1. Suspense fiction
    2. Large type books
    I. Title
    823.9′14 [F]

    ISBN 0–7089–4302–0

Published by
F. A. Thorpe (Publishing)
Anstey, Leicestershire

Set by Words & Graphics Ltd.
Anstey, Leicestershire
Printed and bound in Great Britain by
T. J. International Ltd., Padstow, Cornwall

This book is printed on acid-free paper

1

Monday

Rain was slanting across the café's parking area and wind ruffling its flooded surface as Johnny Parfitt picked his way through the mud, keeping to the lee of the parked wagons wherever possible. He was limping from the discomfort of his sodden shoes, and chilled to a point of misery in wet trousers and a thin mac that clung to him like a black shroud. Finally he was forced to retreat from the weather, one aspect of life which, for four years, had not imposed on his consciousness. He had not been aware of the flaming summer, nor of its final break at the beginning of September. Now it was the end of the month, and still it rained. Johnny had known nothing of that. He had been released from Parkhurst Prison only that morning.

The harsh blare of pop and the sudden blast of warmth at first confused him, but then, so as not to be noticed hesitating at the door, he plunged awkwardly for the counter. It was not yet eleven, and too early for lunch. The café was half empty. The noise was inescapable from the four speakers in the corners.

He bought a mug of tea and cradled it to a remote corner, head low, dark hair slicked and dripping down his neck. With two hands to it, the handle pointing away from him, he gulped at the tea. The eyes of the man two tables away met his. Johnny stared, then looked away.

Then he sat, allowing the heat to soak in. Here he felt comfort, there being fewer customers than he'd feared, and the atmosphere filled him with warm memories. He didn't wish to consider his next move. Decisions were still difficult.

He was a big, gangling man in his mid-thirties, with a long and mournful face, slow to smile but abrupt in his barked laughter. His eyes were deep, but he habitually shaded them with quick movements of his head and a lowering of his eyebrows. The impression was of uncertainty and fear, of insecurity. In practice it was self-protection, though he was not sufficiently intelligent to have analysed it. Far too many people took advantage of him, and his frank eyes revealed his gullibility.

He went for another mug of tea, and on the way back the stranger kicked out a chair in invitation.

'Going far?'

Johnny sat nervously, putting down his mug and moving it around. He shrugged, not replying.

'The name's Kent,' said the man. 'I'm heading north.'

Johnny nodded, and buried his nose in the mug. What had the Governor said? 'Beware of approaches. Until you get back on your feet, you'll be very vulnerable.' Johnny was not quite sure what that meant, but he was certain that he needed a friend. He nodded towards the trailer wagons outside the window.

'You drivin' one of those?'

Kent smiled. 'The new Dodge. Did you notice it?' There was evident pride in his voice.

'Had me head down.'

Kent considered him, nodding slightly. 'You're a driver.' It was a considered opinion.

'Have been. Not now.'

'I can see.'

Johnny grinned suddenly, his face alive. 'I've been standin' out on the road, thumbin' a lift.'

'North?'

Johnny nodded. 'There's no other way from where . . . ' He stopped, and dug his stupid mouth into the mug again.

'Could give you a lift.'

And Johnny avoided his eyes. It was not from suspicion; the man seemed open and friendly. It was from indecision. North certainly, but how far? Branch east to London, and to his parents and his child? Or on to Shropshire — and to Laura? On one side was the powerful and comforting draw of family, on the other was a tangle of emotions that confused and distressed him. Laura might not welcome him. He had not even seen her in court at his trial, and had been more upset by that than by his sentence. But of course, Laura had taken up with Den by then — or the other way round, more like. At that time, the farm would have provided a reasonable hideaway for Den, for a while, and it was possible that he was still there. The last news Johnny had heard of him, he'd certainly been there, dug in, lying low, operating from the farm. But there'd be no welcome from Den, not since that first message from Johnny: *Owe you for a crate of scotch.*

He grimaced at the memory, and Kent said: 'You don't have to, you know.'

'What?'

'Come along with me.'

'It's not that. Depends where.' Johnny looked embarrassed. ''Aven't made up me mind.'

4

'Plenty of time for that.'

So they left together, Kent thrusting his fingers more firmly into his gloves. The rain had eased a little, the wind taking a breath. They skirted the brimming puddles. The clouds moved low, ponderous and unhurried.

'This is it,' said Kent, his feet set wide. He gestured. No amount of nonchalance could bury his pride.

Johnny stood and stared, entranced. The wagon consisted of a ten-wheeled towing unit and an eight-wheeled, forty-foot trailer, with its square load lashed down under a green canvas.

'Twenty tons in that load,' said Kent. 'You ever towed twenty tons?'

Johnny shook his head. Six tons of scotch on an Albion wagon, that'd been his largest — and his last. He couldn't take his eyes from it.

'Well, ain't you gettin' in?'

Johnny walked round and hauled himself into the passenger's seat. The seat had arms! The wonders had no end. He looked round. The cab was spacious, driver's and passenger's seats being separated by a wide, bulging cover, from which the stubby gear-lever rose. Kent caught his glance.

'Got a sixteen-litre diesel under there, mate. Eight-speed box. Can hold seventy on the motorway. No sweat.' He slapped his hands on the wheel, then reached forward for the key, which he'd left in.

Already the glass was steaming. Kent put on the blower. 'Better get that mac off,' he said. 'Stick it down the back.' Then, again: 'The name's Harry.' Reaching.

'My kid's name, that is. Harry. He'll be five, now.'

Kent glanced questioningly at him. The choice of words gave him the clue. 'That's where you're heading — to see the lad?'

But Johnny shook his head, his eyes on the rearing moons of clear glass rising from the heater's blast. He desperately wanted to see his son. But first — yes, surely first — it had to be Laura. Den meant nothing to her, he was sure. Even after all this time, it would be Johnny she wanted.

'If you're going as far as the M4 . . . ' Johnny ventured.

'Sure. Turning east there, for Reading and the Smoke. If we can get through the floods.'

The screen was clear, and they were easing out on to the road. The engine was a live, tense presence at Johnny's elbow. He glanced at his friend. 'There's floods?'

'All over. Hell, mate, where you been?' But his smile suggested he knew.

They drove in silence for a while. Harry

Kent put the radio on, but it seemed to intrude, so he switched it off again. The rain pressed once more on the glass, the wipers fighting it away, and the black, slicked tarmac ran beneath their wheels.

Presently, Kent suggested lunch at a place he knew, a little short of Marlborough. He spoke just as Johnny had been about to confide in him. It would have been rash, Johnny realised, such confidence, but perhaps this friendly little man might realise why Johnny wanted to try again with Laura. He'd go back to her and make everything all right again. Then he'd fetch little Harry back to the farm . . . But there was Den. Always there was Den, and Johnny didn't want violence. The message he sent may have been angry, but now that anger had died. The bitterness had gone; the threat seemed ridiculous, empty. All this he might have explained to Harry Kent, but instead he said:

'Sure. Suits me. They do egg and chips?'

Kent parked immaculately. The surface was tarred. He marched ahead. Rain pattered about them.

They collected their trays. 'Over there,' said Kent. 'By the window.' He spent his life behind glass.

Johnny ate voraciously, his mind racing. The message, seven painfully chosen words, had been smuggled out in his first month at Parkhurst. *Then* they'd been a threat. 'Owe you *for* . . . ' Oh, Den would've known what that meant.

'You're a moody bugger, ain't you?' Kent said suddenly.

'Sorry. Got things on my mind.'

'If you're looking for a job, I could help you. A man like you — your experience — I know somebody who could put something interesting your way. If y'get what I mean . . . '

And Johnny knew just what was meant. He'd been typed. An ex-con. Johnny could guess how he'd be used, and he'd had enough of that. Suddenly he was afraid. Kent could be gently persuasive, and Johnny knew he could offer only a weak response to that.

'I'm finished,' Johnny said. 'You get another coffee, an' I'll go an' fix that cover.' Simply to get away from the smiling, confident Kent.

'What cover?'

'One of your tie-ropes was loose. I'll fix it, and wait in the cab.'

Johnny walked out into the rain. He hurried to the wagon, to treasure as long a period as possible alone with the vehicle. Wagons, you could trust. They could be immensely gentle, yet powerful. Like Johnny himself, if he'd realised.

The trailer was a forty-foot platform with two-foot sides, its load square and solid for another foot above them. A green canvas covered the lot, tied down to hooks along the lower edge of the platform, and it was only the front rope that had come untied. He climbed up, and could see the load, cardboard crates packed neatly, the first one in the near corner displaying its side. 'Black & White', it said. Black & White whisky, it had to mean. Whisky! Johnny snatched at the rope and quickly secured it, as though he had discovered a hidden treasure. Whisky!

He climbed up into the passenger's seat, and was very still. Suddenly he was cold again. *Owe you for a crate of scotch.* Now it was not just the words that came back to him, but the whole scene that had provoked them, with all its brutal clarity. But still there was none of his former hatred for Den.

Then clearly he knew what he was going to do. With one gesture he could take up the ridiculous challenge contained in his message, and convert it to a big joke. Not a crate of scotch, not a dozen crates, but a whole bloody wagon-load, stuck under Den's nose! *Owe you . . .* It'd be a big laugh. Den couldn't help but see that. And Johnny would be escaping from the lure of Harry Kent.

9

He did not work it out logically. His brain only fumbled round with ideas, impressions, but he got there just the same. His basic decision was made.

The keys dangled in the starter switch. It was too much. The temptation to drive this beautiful vehicle was more than he could withstand. He scrambled over the padded engine cover, sat in the driver's seat, placed his hands on the wheel, touched the controls, and knew he could not now turn back from it.

His actions were precise and careful. He started the engine and felt its response beneath his right foot before he made a further move. Then he reached for the gear-lever and eased it into reverse. He idled in the clutch and slowly, eyes darting to each mirror, he backed out the monster that was now his. Then he drove north. Four years of wasted life flowed away, and it was as though they had never been.

He spared no thought for Harry Kent. Parkhurst had bred its own kind of morality: self-preservation. He had once been told that it was not theft unless you expected to keep it. Johnny had not the slightest intention of keeping it. So that was all right, wasn't it.

His subsequent actions were instinctive, arising from lessons learnt in his youth. He had never owned a car, so taking out his girl meant borrowing somebody else's, and then the complex business of evading the police. From this experience Johnny now drew. He drove north — that was where he had told Kent he was heading, and that was where Kent would send them as he saw the truck leaving; but he did not intend even to reach the M4. He took the first reasonable-looking road to the right and kept going until he reached another 'A' road, where he turned right again, right at Hungerford, and thus drove back through Marlborough, but now heading due west. He reckoned that Marlborough was the one place they wouldn't be looking for him.

He realised that a wagon loaded with twenty tons of scotch was likely to attract more attention than the odd car taken for a joyride. So he dodged and twisted, using minor roads once he was through Chippenham, but gradually moving north, and eventually, as the light in the sky slowly faded and the weather began to worsen, he saw that he was close to Worcester. Worcester to Kidderminster, he thought. He was nearly there. But the A449 seemed too big a risk, so he turned left off the main road, not realising he'd made a serious mistake.

The Troughton farm was on the east side

of the river. Laura lived there with her father — and possibly with Den. But Johnny was now working his way north on the west side of the river, with only two miles to go to the next bridge.

He slowed in order to think about it. In this area he was on his own ground, and he could see trouble coming at that bridge. The road from the south required a tight right-hander onto the bridge, which was not very wide anyway, and just over the bridge there was a sharp left-hand turn. Probably huge tractor vehicles with forty-foot trailers managed to negotiate that bridge, but one false move and the wagon would become the centre of attention. Johnny frowned. It was not on.

There was another bridge less than a mile from here, which he and Laura had walked across half a dozen times. It was hardly known, connecting one sub-minor road to another across the river. Josiah Prescott's suspension bridge, that was.

This, too, was narrow, but it had the advantage that it would probably be quite deserted, and Johnny would be able to manoeuvre without attracting attention. He slowed even more, looking for the turn-off down to the bridge. It was no more than a narrow lane, not sign-posted because strictly speaking it was not for general public use.

The bridge had originally been intended as no more than a link between the two halves of Josiah Prescott's estates. Prescott's Folly, they called it around there. But Prescott had committed this folly splendidly in 1837, and it still stood in memory of his enthusiasm, and was still used by the occasional farm wagon and light vehicle.

Prescott had been faced by a problem in that the river, here, was flanked by almost vertical cliffs to a height of a hundred feet. Also, the ground approaching the river from each side had risen steadily. He had therefore cut approach roads into the hillsides, twenty feet lower than the cliff tops, so that they faced each other squarely. These cutaways, though, were only as wide as his bridge, which was fourteen feet. The lane that Johnny was now taking was therefore fourteen feet wide, and curved gently towards the left before reaching the bridge, due to a rock outcrop that Josiah Prescott had not troubled to subdue.

A hundred feet from the bridge, Johnny realised that he was committed. By this time he was easing the massive vehicle along the cutaway at walking pace. Vertical cliffs were pressing in on him from either side, gradually rising higher. The rain had grown heavier still, and strong gusts of wind were driving it against the windscreen. He concentrated every instinct, his eyes darting always to the wing mirrors to be certain the trailer was free.

Then he came in sight of the bridge, and his stomach churned. It seemed so frail, when before, walking across it with Laura, it had seemed firm and strong. Prescott had slung two massive chains from the tops of the cliffs above, beneath which was supported 135 feet of roadway which looked like a slim and flimsy platform. It waited for him, eighty feet above the racing water.

He stopped the vehicle, pawing his face. He felt hot and scared. If the cab had not been so close to the vertical rock surface on his side, he could have opened the door and walked the rest. The rain beat fiercely at his window. To hell with that! He started again. The towing unit shuddered. He rolled the front wheels on to the bridge.

He was now entering the straight line of the bridge platform at a slight angle, and in order to clear the rear wheels of the trailer he had to keep the cab as far over to his right as possible. The out-rigged mirror was the first thing to go. Some instinct told him to keep moving, the speed only a trickle, the cab brushing the hangers on the driver's side.

The bridge platform was stiffened by a four-foot cast-iron parapet in a latticework pattern, and was supported from the chains by iron hangers of one-inch diameter rods at three-feet spacing. For its time the bridge had had a safety margin far beyond its means, but Prescott had not dreamed of over thirty tons on his bridge.

The cab was one third across the bridge when the first hanger bar snapped. It was just behind the cab window, and in the sudden release of its tension it slapped sideways. Johnny heard it strike behind him, but kept going. The rear trailer wheels were clear of the rock edge, and just about to roll on to the bridge.

Then another hanger bar snapped, again on the right, where most of the weight now rested. It cracked like a flayed whip into the side of the cab. The window beside him flew in, and Johnny felt blood on his cheek. The cab was now tilting to the right, and the bridge protested, seeming to writhe with pain. The whole vehicle lurched, and three more hangers parted at the same time.

The cab was in the exact centre of the bridge, the rear of the trailer twenty feet out over the frantic water below. Slowly, like a can crushed in a great hand, Prescott's fancy parapet crumpled up as the right edge of the bridge collapsed, first a foot, then two, then abruptly two more. The brittle cast iron disintegrated, flinging itself sideways, portions hurling themselves at the cab.

The vehicle came to a halt. He was sitting low down at a twenty-degree tilt, and the time had passed when he could expect to move any farther. The headlights slanted up and to the left, on which side only two of the hangers had parted. On the driver's side, as he watched, and as he listened with the engine dead, two more snapped with a hard twang, then with a whine as they broke free. At his elbow another snapped at the point where it entered the platform, and flung itself far out to the right before swinging back, impelled by the taut chain it still clung to, piercing the cab beside Johnny's right foot. It continued on to smash his foot, and finally stopped, wedged beneath the foot pedals.

The bridge was silent at last. Johnny sat whimpering, his breath caught so that he could not cry out. He waited.

The bridge sighed and swung, its centre tilted low to the right, with the massive chain on that side no longer a graceful curve but a notched irregularity. Josiah Prescott's industry proved itself as the metal moaned, but held.

Then, at last, Johnny dared to scream. But the river roared so strongly beneath him that his cries were lost.

2

Tuesday

It was well after one when they located Colin
Marson. He hadn't been asleep; he was lying
on the bunk and listening to the roar of the
rain on the caravan roof. It was still a novelty
to him to be living out in the open, and it still
worried him. Everything worried him. The
pounding of a fist on the caravan door could
only mean more trouble.

The police sergeant was standing in the
mud, slapping gloves into his palm and
looking impatient.

'Are you Marson?' he asked. He had
headed for the largest caravan. 'There's been
an accident at the bridge.'

The assumption was there, that Marson
would come running. The sergeant gestured
to the police car in the shadows behind him,
his mate sitting inside with his mouth to his
radio. He didn't even say which bridge, or
what had happened. Marson had a terrible
premonition that he was referring to Josiah
Prescott's, and scrambled into slacks, donkey
jacket and gum boots. But he insisted on

using the Land-rover. Maybe the sergeant had his orders, but there's such a thing as independence.

They hadn't woken the whole camp. Marson glanced back as they moved away, and all was quiet, not a light in any of the other fifteen caravans. They huddled in the shelter of the pile-driver, with the Kato eighty-ton crane looming behind.

As the evening had progressed, the wind reached storm-force and the rain became torrential. The remote areas of the Midlands were now isolated by severe floods; the relentless gales denied the emergency services access to the bridge by air. Even at only twenty miles from the river, the team employed on the construction of the motor-way had little chance of providing quick, effective assistance. Marson was the leader of the motorway advance team, who were constructing a flyover a good fifteen miles ahead of the main gang. So it was Marson they got — supposedly a man with the resources, the authority and the technical background to face the life-or-death decisions ahead of him. But in these extraordinary circumstances, Marson was chosen for one reason above all others — proximity.

Ahead of the Land-rover they had the winker going, and their siren blasting into the silent and deserted countryside. It niggled at Marson's nerves, so when they got close to the river he was tense, and in no good humour.

And it was Prescott's. He was in an agony of impatience. This bridge, to a civil engineer, was a thing of wonder; one of the first suspension bridges ever built, and not by an engineer, but by a country squire, it was still standing after 150 years. Though working to build the motorway which was set to destroy, Marson had been fighting to preserve it. The cause had been hopeless from the start; now there was no cause left at all.

His first sight of Superintendent Grey was his rigid, inflexible silhouette against the floodlit rain over the river beyond the eastern cliff. Approaching from the east, there was half a mile of heath with a rutted farm road across it, and then, the last quarter of a mile, the grassland began to rise gently towards the water. Prescott — and this was his genius — had seen a way to dispense with the usual support towers for his chains. He had cut approach roads through the cliffs each side of the river, leaving a level road surface each side. This gave him cliffs to each side of his approach roads, twenty feet above their surface, so that he could sling his chains from the cliff tops.

It was a measure for which Marson was full of admiration; but he was all too aware that a century and a half can transform strengths into weaknesses, and weaknesses into strengths.

When Marson arrived they had a fire appliance crouched in the last few yards of the approach road, with a floodlight centred on the bridge. Behind it there was a whole gaggle of police cars, together with an unhappy-looking farm tractor. The police car swung left onto the stubble grass before reaching the cutaway, and pulled in. Marson drove on past it and up the steep incline to the police officer on the heights. Grey had taken a position on the eastern cliff edge, only a few feet from the low masonry pile over which one of Prescott's chains was still firmly straining.

Marson saw a man faced with an appalling problem, with little clue as to how to handle it. As he got down from the Land-rover, Grey approached him. Marson thought he saw some degree of relief in his movement, though something in his expression indicated that he'd expected an older person than Marson, someone flaunting his authority and experience like a pair of hoisted flags. Whatever his reason, Grey chose to be abrupt.

'So, you're here at last,' he said, lifting his chin.

Marson moved as close as possible to the cliff edge and shielded his eyes from the rain.

One glance was enough. 'What d'you want from me?'

Impatience hardened his tone. The situation was hopeless, he saw. The two main chains were still intact, the up-river one from the cliff the other side of the cutaway still almost retaining its line. This side — and he could now see why Grey had chosen this position — had a whole scatter of hangers broken, so that the beautiful run of the down-river chain was broken and notched. Marson could have wept. The bridge platform was a wreck, broken into a deep 'V' at the down-river side, with half its parapet gone and the other half piled against the wagon's cab.

And there it sat, a blasted huge trailer vehicle, which nobody in his right mind would have brought onto that bridge. The front of the trailer and the rear of the tow unit were tilted into the bottom of the V, poised on the very edge of the drop, with the river racing and roaring eighty feet below. All rigidity was gone. The bridge platform didn't even reach the roadways each side of the river; ten feet or more had disappeared each end.

What he was looking at was an isolated unit, swinging there, swaying in a wind that ran erratically down the river — less forceful than before but less predictable also — creaking and sighing and making a low keening sound of metal in distress. Marson watched its agony. With each swing he expected the whole thing to break away. The policeman replied:

'Well . . . what can we do?'

Rain dripped from the peak of his cap and his raincoat. He loomed over Marson, all suppressed urgency, and making little movements of tension with his hands. He expected an instant reply.

'Nothing.' Marson was crisp. 'Stand and look at it long enough, and it'll do it without any help.' He knew what he was saying. He'd made many exploratory surveys of those cliffs before. 'I can get a team with flame-cutters, and dump the thing. Before it's too late.'

Grey jerked his head. The close-trimmed moustache glistened with moisture. 'We can't do that . . .'

'It'll be insured,' said Marson sourly. The truck — but not the bridge.

'What about the driver, damn it?'

Marson was used to dealing with materials and forces and angles. It had not occurred to him that he was being called in to save a life. But now it was all too clear: with a gap at either side, there can have been no way for the driver to escape. He tried to hide his mistake: 'Any idiot who drives a thing like that onto there deserves all . . . '

But Grey had turned away and marched a few paces, gathering himself.

Marson stared at the bridge attentively. The concentration of light was catching spears in the driving rain. Now he could detect that there was no glass in the driver's door. It was on the down-wind side, but all the same he couldn't hold back a shudder. Late September, and the rain bit like ice crystals in the north wind.

Grey returned to his side, contained and cold. 'What about a helicopter? I could call up a team.'

'It's the wind.' Marson waved an arm loosely at the area over the bridge. Grey didn't seem to get the point. 'The gusts are coming straight down the river. They get caught between the cliffs and — woof — they'd throw a chopper to hell and away.'

Grey looked at him anxiously. 'You've got special equipment, on call?'

Marson avoided the question. 'Is he alive?'

'We don't know. There's been no movement.'

'Then hadn't we better find out? That's the first job, surely.'

'I've sent for a doctor,' said Grey. 'The floods have cut us off from all the major hospitals. The weathermen say it'll clear up, eventually. But there's no chance of a paramedic, not for at least twenty-four hours. One of my lads said he knew the local GP, knew where he was tonight. He's on his way. You get him down there and — '

'Nobody's going down there. Not one foot set on that bridge. Can't you feel it? Spit on it and it'd go.'

'Then how the hell do we find out? If he's alive, we have to keep him alive.'

Marson always told himself that he could never resist a challenge. As he stood looking out at the bridge, Grey's urgency forcing him to answer, he realised that by that he had always meant a challenge on paper, back in his office where everything had a solution. Here and now, there could be no guarantees.

'I don't know,' he said. 'I don't know.'

The number of times he'd stood on this very spot. The hours he'd spent, just looking at the bridge, marvelling at its beauty, and wondering how a concrete single-span could ever replace it. He wouldn't have argued that Prescott's suspension bridge was a master-piece of engineering. For one thing, Prescott's chains were a dozen times stronger than he'd needed. But Darby had cast them — along with the fancy parapet — for him at Coalbrookdale, and perhaps Darby had been recalling what he'd done for Telford and his Menai Bridge, maybe had still been brooding over his own wonderful triumph with the Ironbridge. But certainly, those chains would hold, Marson was certain of that. There was a chance they'd hold too damned well. Marson knew those cliffs, as Prescott himself could not have done. He'd made soundings and taken bores. What he was standing on was argillaceous rock, and it made the problem a hundred times worse than it appeared to Grey. But Marson said nothing. It was too early to admit defeat.

'And anyway,' said Grey, having another go at him, 'you daren't dump the bridge. Even if he's dead.'

'Why not?' Marson asked, lifting his chin.

Grey turned and made a dramatic gesture up-river, flinging out his arm. 'That's Lower Prescott, a mile up there. It's called Lower because it's right down at river level. Not much of a township, but people live there. You might not appreciate that, living on motorways.' He could be bitter when he tried. 'And with all this rain they're close to a flood, as you might guess. Not just the town, but the whole countryside. Thousands of acres of farmland. The river's high — higher than ever, they reckon. It narrows through here, where the cliffs close in. So, drop that wagon and the bridge in there . . . ' He allowed it to tail off, shaking his head, one rim of light from the edge of the floodlights catching the hard line along his jaw. 'You understand?'

Marson moved closer to the cliff edge. Down there, chopped off by the concentration of light, it was black, dead black. But he could hear it, the thunder and tumble of the water. He even imagined he could feel the spray, a hundred feet above it. Certainly he could sense the vibration. But the edge-to-edge reach between the cliffs was 135 feet. He knew that. The wagon and trailer couldn't have been more than fifty feet.

He stepped back. 'No.' He forced some semblance of certainty into his tone. 'That lot — it all looks solid and heavy, but it couldn't make much difference.'

'You're too damned confident,' Grey said suspiciously.

It was what Marson had to be, what he'd trained for. You weigh the different pressures and loads, and you decide. Then you go ahead. It had to be like that. Uncertainty could lead only to inaction. He was paid for making it work that way.

'We might not have too long to wait, then we'll know,' Marson grunted. 'I'll have to radio back,' he said, as though for something to do. He turned away and climbed into the Land-rover, chasing the trails of half-glimpsed ideas through his brain. He was struggling to form even the most rudimentary plan of action, but he knew that whatever strategy he was to adopt, the basic materials would be the same. And he knew that, sometimes, having the materials could make the strategy present itself more quickly.

All the motorway teams were linked by radio. They operated miles from phone lines, and the few mobiles were unevenly spread out. Marson's man would be asleep, if he had any sense. It took ten seconds for him to answer, and the voice was only half awake.

'Yeah . . . yeah?'

'It's Marson.' Marson had been trying to wean them off the archaic 'mister,' but it was hard going. 'I'm at Prescott's Bridge. Prescott's. You got that? Write it down.'

'Got it.'

'Dig out Jeff and four of the welders. Tell Jeff I'll need the Kato, and . . . ' Marson snapped his fingers, forgetting the crane operator's name.

'Tony,' said the voice.

'That's him. Six men in the back-up truck.

Better throw a canvas over it — it's pouring down. And flame-cutting torches. Large bottles and small. Some cable. Half-inch. Around a hundred metres. A hundred yards, then.' He'd heard muttering.

'I know what a metre is, Mr Marson.' The voice was flat.

'Fine. As soon as they can. Straight here. Tell Jeff it's an emergency.'

The voice was calm. 'Got it. Over and out.'

'Now what?' asked Grey, as Marson climbed down again.

'Contingency plans. Can you clear that approach road for us. I'll need the fire engine out — they can go home as far as I'm concerned.'

'I'll move them out. But I won't send them home just yet, if that's okay by you.'

'Whatever. As long as you can get them out of my way, you can stand the firemen on each other's heads for all I care. I need a clear run right to the edge.'

'You've got something in mind?'

Marson did not have too much in mind, but he knew that he would have. He was trying not to give in too easily, was doing his best to be seen to act decisively and with conviction. It was simpler to ignore Grey's question than to give himself away with a specific lie. He carried on as though Grey hadn't spoken. Grey began to turn away, to set his own men moving. Marson called after him.

'You *did* send for a doctor?'

Grey didn't pause or answer. His shoulders stiffened as he walked away, with the light catching glints from the insignia on his raincoat shoulders.

Marson turned from the bridge. He couldn't bear to keep watching, when any second there might be a shift of load that could touch off a pressure reaction. Prescott had designated it a toll bridge, he recalled. It had required an Act of Parliament, and he'd been allowed to charge a toll of one halfpenny. Not that anybody had ever paid it. In the end the bridge had been presented to posterity — and now it was dying. He turned his back to it, feeling sick. The wagon was its final toll.

It was too early to expect the distant headlights of the Kato hydraulic crane, though it would do thirty on a good road. The countryside fell away before him, with only a distant pin-point here and there breaking the black velvet night. He realised that there should have been at least a throwback of light from the floods, turned, and saw that the fire appliance was backing out of the cutting.

Now the wagon out over the river was dark, and seemed more threatening. He climbed into the Land-rover, started up, and with his head out of the window edged it forward in low-low until the front wheels were beginning to run on to the fall-off to the cliff edge. He watched the line of the headlights canting down, rolling the tyres an inch at a time, cursing the spray of light for shooting out above the cab, glancing at the tyres, urging the light downwards. He got the handbrake locked on, grabbed his binoculars, and jumped out. He had the cab illuminated again.

With the binoculars, the raindrops were enlarged in blurred unfocus and screened his vision. He could see no sign of anybody in the cab. Perhaps . . . and he paced a few yards as he examined the thought . . . perhaps there was a chance that the driver had got out of the cab, stumbled, and now lay on the rocks below. For a moment he prayed that this could be so.

Way down on the heath a car's lights were fumbling off the roadway. He tried the glasses, but it was still no good. Carried on the wind he could hear the distant slam of the door. And then he waited, eyes straining for movement. Even in the dark it was possible to detect something stirring, however slightly.

He thought he saw a flick of white against the darkness, then a shadow became a man, and he came on up, walking firmly and purposefully. And at last stood in front of Marson.

He was not in the least short of breath. He loomed over Marson, at least six feet of him, a broad man, leaning forward, head tilted and hand holding a black hat on his head. The flash of white had been his silk scarf. He was in evening dress, black tie, frilled and lacy shirt, black pumps, a loose mac thrown over it all, and he was carrying a doctor's bag.

'What a hell of a time to grab hold of somebody,' he complained. The voice was hearty. It would plough through complaints and protests with its message of confidence. 'They said you were up here, but what . . .' He turned sideways as the wind blustered. The back-throw from the headlights caught his face for a moment. It was the large, lumpy conglomerate of a boxer. 'I'd got this girl,' he went on. 'We'd been to a do. I'd about got it made. We reached my place in the square, and this copper had to go and step in . . . I could've killed him. Ten more minutes . . . Okay. So what've we got? Where's the patient?'

Marson stepped to one side. This was a character who'd have no patience for build-ups. He allowed him to see for himself.

The doctor came up beside him and stared a long, long time at the bridge. Slowly he raised his arms and used both hands to shade his eyes. Marson moved his bag to safety, and stood waiting.

'He's down there?' No heartiness now.

'Where else could he be? We haven't seen any movement.'

'But you can't expect . . . ' The doctor's voice sounded hoarse.

'I've got binoculars, if you want to try them.'

The gesture was an angry dismissal, and he turned with it, throwing his head back. 'Oh, this is great! What am I supposed to do? Clamber down that chain, bag in one hand and stethoscope in the other? Peek in at the window, say: 'You all right, old chap?' and toss him a couple of aspirins?'

It was a brave effort. He nearly achieved the correct tone of dismissive flippancy, but there was a sense of breathlessness, and his eyes were hunting, anywhere but to meet Marson's.

Marson said quickly: 'It wasn't what I had in mind.'

'Then what?'

'We've got to know if he could be alive.'

'How the hell . . . ' Then he moved

restlessly, shoulders forward, the bulking advance of a prop forward, searching the opposition for weaknesses. 'I can't tell you anything from here,' he said at last, his voice in control.

'As I'd guessed.'

'So what . . . ?'

'I don't know. I'm telling you the truth, now. I can't see any way, at this stage, to get anybody to him.'

'Then there's nothing I can do.'

'But it'd be useful if you'd hang around until I'm sure.'

The doctor was eyeing him with uncertainty. There had been no dismissal of the ridiculous idea that he would, in some terrifying way, be transported onto that bridge. 'Then I'll wait in my car.'

'Could be a long wait.' No definite plan had yet been decided. 'I'm Colin Marson,' he said. 'Chief Engineer and site boss with one of the motorway teams.'

Then the doctor smiled and his eyes disappeared in their pouches. He stuck out his hand. 'Chris Keene.'

'We'll bring him to you,' Marson promised, with nothing to back it up. 'I hope to lift him off there and drop him at your feet. There's a crane coming. A big one. And there's just one slim chance . . .'

'Have I got time to get home and change?' Keene asked. 'Just in case.'

Marson smiled at the childlike eagerness. 'We'll be at least an hour setting up.'

Keene turned, and began to walk down to his car. Marson shouted after him: 'Make that an hour and a half.'

That was in case the girl had waited. Marson turned back to the bridge. It was still there.

He was alone and free from possibility of interruption. A plan to lift the driver clean off the bridge had already begun to form, and the details were coming to him one by one, filling in the gaps in their own short time. But there remained one crucial factor for him to assess. He reached inside the Land-rover for his rubber-cased torch. The point where he was standing was a few yards to the left of the squat masonry pile over which Josiah Prescott had his chain running. Twenty feet farther back it was anchored into the naked rock. Superintendent Grey had spoken of the danger of flooding if the bridge and wagon fell into the river, but Grey couldn't appreciate the full danger. Marson crouched and directed the torch onto the rock surface.

There was no grass layer to soften the rock on the peaks. Here it was grey, slimy with the rain, its corrugations running in line with the river. Marson glanced sideways, at the chain and its low support, and searched with the torch for what he had feared. He found it.

The crack was small, and might not have been noticed in the ridged surface. Marson put his finger on it, concentrating, and felt it move. Again he glanced sideways at the chain, which consisted of huge iron links, eighteen inches long and a foot across. It moved restlessly on its support, groaning. But the chain was safe; it was the cliff that was in danger.

3

Chris Keene stumbled down from the cliff, his feet soggy in their thin pumps, his brain in turmoil. Make no mistake about it, he told himself, there *had* been a suggestion that he would have to go down to that wagon. He had been temporarily released, to go away and contemplate what horrors Marson might have in mind for him.

He found his Maestro, which was now surrounded by police cars and other vehicles. He couldn't see the fire engine anywhere.

In the square of Lower Prescott he had his surgery, with a couple of rooms over it. It was not much of a practice, but he didn't really need one. Not for the money; his aunt had been generous in her Will. But his father had started it, and a chap had to do something to justify his existence, he supposed. He would not have called himself a dedicated doctor, unaware that his patients had a different opinion. He had permission to leave his car round the rear of the Crown, and walking back from there, deep into the hush of the night, he could hear the rush of the river across the end of High Street, a couple of hundred yards away. Back there, on the cliffs, it had sounded angry, but at town level it was positively menacing. He paused to listen, worried, and noticed the light on in Frank Allison's office opposite. Then, as he stared at it, it went out.

He waited, and as Allison closed his street door he called out: 'Hey, Frank.'

Allison looked startled, then saw who it was and walked across the square. It was not really a square, just that the shops were set back a few more yards around there.

'You're up late,' Allison said. It was no more than a comment.

'You too,' Chris said, and it was a criticism.

Allison grimaced, and shook his head. He was carrying an umbrella but seemed to have forgotten to open it. Typical. Frank Allison was as tall as the doctor, and about half his weight, and Chris had been watching him fade away over the past two years, watching with professional and personal concern. Allison was around ten years older than Chris, but they had been close friends for a long time. Now Allison looked haggard and drawn.

'I've been drafting a petition,' he said, quietly proud.

'Not another. You're too late, Frank.'

'We've got to fight this, and go on fighting,'

Allison said, in his quiet, aggravated tone. 'We can't let the motorway come through.'

His eyes were burning with the internal flame of the fanatic. Chris tried to make light of the obsession.

'We've done it all,' he reminded him. 'For two years or more. Appeals and Committees and Referees. It's coming, Frank. Hell, it's closer than you seem to realise.'

'Fight on . . . '

'But would it be such a bad thing? Taken all told — would it really? Look, come up for a minute and have a drink.'

'No,' Allison said. 'I'll get on home.'

'I'll drive you.' He knew Allison walked the mile north along the river road.

'I'd rather walk. There're things to think about. I'm basing this petition on the historical significance of Prescott's Bridge. It's a new approach. You know they intend to take it down . . . '

'Frank, it's *coming* down. Right now.'

It was as good as striking him. This business had got into Frank's veins, that was the trouble. Like an injected drug. It had all started casually enough, years back. It seemed a lifetime ago now, when the motorway had been just a suggestion, and Frank had been elected by the locals to represent them and their livelihoods, just because he was their only solicitor. And because he'd do it free. But it had got hold of him. He didn't donate just his fees; he gave all of himself, flesh and bones and stubborn soul. He had made his name — and his money — drawing up contracts for small businesses, tightening and exploiting loopholes beyond the question of honour. But he gave up everything for the community. It became a full-time job, and he was forced to live off his savings. Trips here and there to dig out expert witnesses, briefing counsel, the lot. He beavered away, and the appeal was beaten every way he turned. But he refused to give in. Because it had become a fetish, Chris reckoned, because it was his life. And now, when the motorway was only a few miles away, when nothing could deflect it short of an atom bomb, he had to think up the wild idea of having the bridge declared an historical monument.

'It's what?' Allison demanded, his face limp, looking stupid for a second.

'There's been an accident,' Chris told him. 'The bridge is wrecked, whatever happens.'

'I'll have to go and see.'

'You can't do anything.'

'All the same, I'll have to see.'

Allison couldn't keep still, all jittery. There was a nervous breakdown coming on, or

Chris'd tear up his degree. 'Come inside a minute, Frank. You need a night's rest. I'll give you something.'

'No, Chris,' Allison said. 'It's very thoughtful of you, but you know I can't do that. I'll get off.'

Chris tried a last appeal, because Allison was turning away. 'Then at least let me run you up to the bridge.'

Allison paused, looking back, smiling that smile Chris had always loved to see, but which now made him feel empty.

'You look a mess, Chris,' he said solemnly. 'Go and get a bath, then *you* go to bed.'

Chris watched him walk away, wondering what he could shout that would fetch him back. Allison's umbrella was still furled. He was walking with tired, hunched shoulders, his feet dragging. Allison was the embodiment of the community. He was heading for the bridge, and Chris wondered whether he'd even notice the level of the racing river, which threatened them far more than the motorway.

He nearly trod on the sodden cat. He was always around. Seemed to think he lived there. Chris would've booted him off, if he'd owned any boots. It followed Chris up the stairs, and didn't smell sweet. He'd been catting again. Chris shut him in the kitchen with his dinner, and went to change, then

40

forgot to throw him out again when he ran downstairs in old jeans and a parka, and his cleated hill-climbers. The place would stink to high heaven when he returned.

He couldn't think why he was in such a hurry to get back to the cliff. Well, of course he'd given it some thought since the first sight. Who wouldn't? There had never been anything he hadn't been able to face. Then they'd stuck the bridge under his nose, and the suggestion was there that somehow he'd get down there, or be got there. He didn't understand what had happened to him then, except in a theoretical sense. It wasn't something solid and physical he could go at, that was the point. It was just danger. Cold danger. He had been afraid, and for a moment his mind had gone into a tangle.

It was a new experience to him. He was not even certain he remembered it correctly, and now was anxious to get another look at the bridge, to check on his original reactions.

So he raced the journey back, and very nearly drove into the back of their crane.

Such a huge thing. It blocked the road, and was doing about twenty at the time. He had to drift along in its diesel fumes for almost a mile. It had two cabs, one for driving it and one for operating the boom, which was a squat retracted bulk along its top. That

Marson character obviously had something special in mind, Chris thought, his confidence blooming.

'We'll bring him to you,' Marson had said. Dump him at his feet. Well, that sounded all right, and clearly this crane was the instrument they'd be using.

So he followed it patiently. Nothing was going to happen until it got there.

There seemed to be a lot more cars around when he arrived. The news had got about. In the dead of night. Marvellous, he thought. He parked off the road and walked on to the cliff top.

They had run the crane right along the cutting, and where the cliffs rose each side there was only a few feet of clearance for its huge wheels. They had left ten feet of roadway in front of it, and there were a couple of swivel spotlights above its cab, aimed at the bridge. On that end patch of roadway there was a small group, waving their arms around in brisk discussion, and chasing shadows into the cone of floodlit rain. The wind howled and hissed across the end gap, and they were standing only three feet from the absolute edge. Chris had to scramble over the bodywork of the crane in order to hear what was going on.

He had met Superintendent Grey once or

twice before, having done some work for the police. Grey he knew as a solid, reliable man, a bit grim perhaps, humourless and inflexible. Grey was saying something about the driver stranded on the bridge. Chris hung back.

' . . . now know that he pinched the thing down south. Obviously, he cut through here to evade our cars . . . '

They seemed to take no notice of Grey. Standing beside Marson was a taller man with grey in his hair and a grave face, who was nodding and nodding, but saying nothing. Marson called him Jeff. Jeff was wearing one of those slickers that ship's captains use, and what must have been thigh-length boots, otherwise the rain would have poured down into his socks. Between them, looking from one face to the other, all perky attention, was a smaller man in his late twenties, with a plastic red-and-white cap perched on his curly mass of hair. He had a knobbly face and small hands, and a wide mouth.

'Tony,' Marson said to him, 'that cab's around seventy feet from here. What's your lift at that radius?'

'Six tons,' said Tony.

'There's not going to be much to spare. Look: the wind — the thing's swaying. How'll the boom handle, out there over the bridge?

Always remembering that you can't use your outriggers.'

Tony grimaced. He knew what he could and couldn't do. 'I can manage.'

'But I mean — '

'He can manage,' Jeff cut in flatly. 'What'd you got in mind?'

Marson jerked his head towards the bridge. 'We can't lift the whole lorry with the Kato — we'd need a much bigger machine for that. But the cab on its own can't weigh much more than a few tons. Those big wagon units — you can't see, because of all the parapet stuff against the front, but some of them have cabs that hinge forward. Access to engine, or some such thing. Maybe this one's like that. The seats hinge up with the shell. So . . . I thought . . . ' He glanced around the faces, uncertain for one moment, then he plunged on. 'This is what we do. Get down to that bridge — gently, Tony, very gently you understand — '

'Will do.' Tony nodded, his eyes on the bridge.

' — with a gas cutting torch and some bottles, and cut the slabs of parapet away, then if there are any hinges, cut them out, get a chain on the cab, and lift the whole lot out.'

There was a short silence. Grey tried again to make his point. 'He stole the thing. It's got a load of twenty tons of whisky.'

'Looks tricky,' said Jeff stolidly. Grey might as well not have been there.

'Of course it's tricky. But what else is there?'

Marson waited stubbornly for the silence to end.

'There's nothing else,' said Jeff in a gruff voice. The impression was that he knew that tone, and resented it.

'All right then. So you lay that on, Jeff. The small gas bottles, a cutting torch. Some way of slinging the stuff over my shoulders — '

'You're not going?' said Jeff.

'Who else?' Marson demanded. 'I can't *tell* anybody — '

'Then I'm coming with you.'

Marson opened his mouth, then paused. One of the crane's lights edged on to his face. His lips were drawn back. Then he spoke quietly. 'I'm capable of using a flame cutter, Jeff.'

'I know you are. But I can do it better. Quicker. There can't be much time to spare.'

'And no weight to spare at all.'

'That wagon must weigh thirty tons. One extra man's not — '

'I was going to get there with my foot in the hook. Two'd need some sort of a rig, a seat, something like that.'

Then Jeff smiled, almost sadly. 'I've got Cropper rigging it right now.'

Marson knew it was sensible. He plunged his hands into his pockets. A gust of rain flinched his head sideways.

'Very well,' he conceded. 'Let's get on with it. Where's Cropper?'

'He's coming.'

Chris could hear somebody scrambling over the side of the vehicle behind him. He moved out of the way, and thus into the light.

'Ah, here you are, Chris,' said Marson, cheerfully enough. But he was uneasy. 'This is Jeff Fisher, the site foreman. And Tony . . . ' He groped for the surname. Chris covered it by murmuring how-d'you-dos.

'I've met the super,' he said.

'You here, Keene?' asked Grey.

'They're going to get him out for me,' Chris told him. Hopefully, that was.

Jeff said: 'You got everything, Cropper? Good man.'

Cropper was a squat, round hunk of muscle with a dull-looking face. He peered from one to the other uncertainly. He was about to speak, but Marson cut in, tension catching his voice.

'Come on, Cropper, let's have it rigged.'

It was a signal for Tony to dive for his

operating cab. Maybe he was simply getting clear of what might have been an explosion from Cropper. There certainly didn't seem to be much comprehension in his expression. He was a bulky ape of a man, who wouldn't possess the subtlety to recognise Marson's tension. For a moment he looked confused, then Tony had the boom projecting, almost vertically, and was lowering the hook. It fell with a clatter at Cropper's feet — a gentle hint — before it lifted again to eye level.

What Cropper had rigged was a four-foot board, a foot across, with holes in its corners, through which he'd fastened ropes. He'd looped them over the hook. The small platform swung two feet from the road surface. Chris stared at it, and swallowed.

They took their positions, side by side, and Cropper loaded the gas bottles between them. These were connected by rubber pipes to the cutting torch. Jeff signalled. Marson was gripping the rope with white knuckles. Chris was beginning to realise that Marson was a desk man, a theoretician. This would be agony for him, but he couldn't back away from it.

Then, with a smoothness and speed that was startling, the flimsy platform lifted, and at once was extended outwards. The wind caught it. For a moment a sheet of rain obscured the two men, then they were shooting over the bridge, tiny and lost, and completely vulnerable. Lord, Chris was glad it wasn't him.

4

Marson had to convince himself he'd made the correct decision. They were the best combination, Jeff and himself. Jeff could handle any piece of equipment on the site, and Marson was the one to consider the stresses and opposing forces, and make decisions on his calculations.

He hadn't reckoned on the abrupt surge into the full force of the wind. The boom projected them rapidly, and the chair bucked and swayed so that for a moment he thought they were going to lose the torch and the gas bottles. But Jeff was calm, and sat with one hand securing the equipment and the other to one of the ropes, while Marson grabbed frantically for both of them his side. Then the upheaval ceased when they were over the vehicle, the rain was on their backs, and he could spare time to assess the situation.

From vertically above, the wagon occupied one side of the bridge, its off-side, and was thrust into a shallow V. The driver's side of the cab seemed to be hanging over the shattered edge of the bridge's platform. The whole thing was swaying, though not to their own rhythm, and now that they were closer the creaking of the chain was quite distinct. Marson couldn't see what was preventing the wagon from plunging into the river. He said: 'Signal him down.'

Because the bridge surface at its centre was well below its original level, there was quite a way to go. Tony fed out more cable, and they dropped slowly, but with the extra length there was more influence from the wind. To Marson it seemed that they could be dashed to pieces at any moment.

'He's not going to do it,' he said.

Jeff grunted. 'Tony knows.'

Tony was making small sideways movements with the boom, playing them like a trout fly for the gentle let-down. Marson held his breath, staring down one moment at the cab roof, the next on what was left visible of the platform surface. Then a hand seemed to catch them, steady the chair, and drop it smoothly to the roadway. They plunged away from it, and stood with straddled legs.

Marson saw at once that it was worse than he'd anticipated. With the fracturing of the cast-iron parapet along each side, the platform had completely lost its rigidity. Looking down its length he could see it writhing as though in pain, cracks opening and closing and the surface layer of tarmac tossed up in great, heaving flakes. The front cab unit had its rear wheels thrust down into the lowest point of the V, nose up, and was over at an angle of fifteen degrees, leaning away from them. Piled against it were slabs of the wrecked parapet, up over the cab, though some miracle had preserved the windscreen. Beyond the vehicle, the support hangers had whole sections already broken, and those remaining were quivering with strain.

They had to bend sideways to prevent themselves from sliding down against the cab.

'Where do we start?' shouted Jeff, his face strained.

Then Marson realised the intensity of the noise. It was a constant jumbled howl of tortured steel, of scraping and whining, and came from all round them.

'I'm going to take a look in the cab,' he called back.

Jeff nodded, braced his foot against the front wheel, and helped Marson up. The cab was leaning away from him, and he was spreadeagled across the passenger's door. He tried to open it, but it was warped, and locked solid. He hefted himself higher. He took his rubber torch from his pocket and held it out.

The driver had slipped down into the far corner, hunched low down against his door, his head just below the shattered side screen. He had dark, massed hair, with a strange white streak through it. Marson couldn't be sure, but he thought he caught a glimpse of the left eye. One finger seemed to move on the driver's left knee. Marson realised it was pointing, so followed the direction downwards with the torch's ray.

Way down amongst the pedals there was a tangle of metal. Marson couldn't see how much of it involved the right foot, but certainly it was trapped. Mangled and trapped. He shouted something, though the driver would never have heard, then slid down and leaned panting against the cab.

'Get him out, Jeff, for Christ's sake!' he shouted.

Beneath their feet the whole thing was flexing. Every inch of the metal cried out to the changing stresses. Sweat began to trickle down Marson's spine.

Jeff had his head down, trying to catch a light to his cutting torch. He struck match after match before the orange light flamed in a cloud of black smoke, then he turned on the oxygen and the cone became blue and pointed. Marson couldn't hear its roar.

'Here!' he shouted. 'There and there.' Pointing out places to cut.

This was the first part of the operation, to

cut the slabs of parapet from in front of the nose of the cab. Jeff was standing with his right leg bent, bracing down with his left, something of Marson's frantic urgency seeming to have communicated. He worked fast. Marson indicated the most effective positions, the thinnest, the most vulnerable. His brain was racing as he computed stresses and strains. As the sections came free, he threw them out over the river, releasing the hot metal quickly.

They were working with intense concentration. Marson no longer called the directions, merely stabbed his finger — there, there. But the change was noticeable. They both paused at the same instant, heads raised.

All around them the clamour had altered, had intensified. It came from no particular point, but flooded in on them. Abruptly, Marson realised the truth.

They had been permitted to place their feet on it, their weight. But the equilibrium had been finely balanced, and part of it had consisted of the parapet slabs they had been cutting away. There had come a point where the balance was destroyed, and the bridge rejected them. Grumbling, it flexed its strength, and reached for its weakest points.

Their eyes met. Startled, Jeff turned off the torch. Marson realised he was shouting at the top of his voice, but the sound was lost. There was a shrill howl embracing them. It rose higher, then terminated, when Marson thought he could stand it no longer, in an explosion of collapse.

The bridge bucked under their feet. Marson groped frantically for the cab unit's front wheel, looked down, and saw it rise from the tarmac, an inch, two inches, and remain poised. He felt they were falling sideways. There was a growl, the metal not being satisfied. The forces nudged each other, shuffled, and complained in plaintive whines all along the length of the bridge.

Then the new equilibrium was established. The wheel gently set itself down on the tarmac surface. The platform shuddered beneath their feet.

At last there was nothing but the sway and the sigh. Marson's hearing was concentrated on it, every other sense withheld. He heard one sound, cutting through it.

It was a scream. It had gone on beyond the rest, persisting, but it, too, gradually died away, with Marson straining for it because he knew it proved the driver was still alive.

'Signal him down!' he shouted.

5

Chris could not move. He had his hand clamped on the rim of one of the crane's floodlights, and behind him the diesel was throbbing. His eyes were on the bridge. He watched it jerk and throb. For a moment he was sure it had gone, then the two men stood out clear and sharp again, struggling to keep their feet on its surface.

The genius in the cab above his head was juggling with the boom as though it was a kid's cane with his bait dangling from it. The man called Jeff was reaching for the chair, missing, reaching again, then he'd got one knee on it and was hauling himself onto the surface. For a moment Chris lost sight of Marson, then he saw him struggling to his feet, and Jeff lay face-down on the board, one hand stretched down to his boss.

It seemed that Tony linked the hands. Jeff drew Marson from the bridge onto the chair, and suddenly the boom was up and away, with the chair twisting and tossing as he hauled it in. He dropped them gently on the road surface, and they scrambled apart.

Grey put a hand to Marson's elbow, but he

was pushed away. Jeff stood with his head hanging for a moment. Marson was swaying on his feet, his face full in the flush of light, the channels down from his nose engraved. Grey offered his cigarettes. Marson fumbled one out and struggled to light it, then drew deeply on it, his head back, the smoke in his teeth. He gestured with it.

'I said, didn't I? Not one foot on it, I said.'

'You heard?' Jeff asked quietly. He was reaching out an old, black pipe.

Marson glanced away. 'Yes.'

'He screamed,' said Jeff, staring at his fingers as he stuffed the pipe.

'He's alive. We'll have to get you to him, Doctor. We certainly can't get him out.'

'Have to?' Chris asked. Nice of Marson to have made the decision. That fear was back again. 'To him?'

Grey put in: 'But you just said: nobody to go on that bridge.'

'Not on it,' said Marson. 'There could be another way. Let's get out of this bloody rain. We've got to talk about this, have a conference.'

Grey refused to accept the sound of a scream in all that noise. 'Did you actually see him? Really there, and moving about?'

Marson began to push past him, then paused. 'Yes, I saw him. Over against the driver's door. I thought I saw a finger move. He's alive, Grey. A youngish chap. Long face. Dark hair with a kind of white streak. Got all that down?'

Grey was making clucking noises, apologising for having been misunderstood. Chris thought he heard a muffled cry of distress from behind him. He turned, but the floodlight completely blinded him. Then he distinctly heard a voice speak in choked appeal.

'Johnny!' It was a woman's voice, on an intake of breath.

He moved round the light, but couldn't see anything. His eyes were still blinded. There were stumbling sounds, then silence.

When he turned back, Tony had climbed down to join the group. Jeff had an arm round his shoulders and was thumping him. 'That was great, Tony. Lovely work.' And the youngster smiled in delight as they turned away together. Marson called after them.

'You'd better be there, Jeff. We'll get together in the back-up truck. In a quarter of an hour.' As Jeff and Tony scrambled back over the crane's bodywork, Marson realised it was too late to offer Tony his own congratulations and thanks. 'Christ, but I could do with a cup of tea,' he said.

'This back-up truck,' Chris said. 'How do I

know it?' He had to be in on this meeting; he didn't dare to turn his back on it in case they planned something for him he couldn't handle.

'Green canvas cover,' Marson said. 'You can't miss it.'

Chris turned away, and went searching for her.

Behind the crane it was very dark. A few headlights swept across the heath, went out, flashed on. Engines revved. On the cliff tops, Grey's men stood guard, well back from the edge. There were now enough sightseers, even though it was three o'clock, to make vigilance necessary. He walked rapidly along the road towards his car. He had a dozen bottles of brown ale on the back seat.

She was sitting in a battered old Mini, only a few yards from his own Maestro. He knew she was the one by her stillness, and by the fact that she was simply sitting, staring forward and yet clearly not seeing him. He stopped, and tapped the side window. She jerked round, startled.

'Can I have a word with you?' he asked, mouthing it.

She was frozen, and a turning car threw light into her wide, huge eyes. He opened the passenger's door.

'I'm Doctor Keene,' he introduced himself,

smiling, trying to put her at her ease. 'I'd like to talk to you. Just for a minute.'

She looked away, but didn't tell him to go to hell, so he took that as a welcome and slid in beside her. She had her hands passive in her lap, the fingers curled up like a child.

'It was you, wasn't it, up there?' he asked gently. 'Do you know him?'

'His name's Johnny Parfitt,' she told him, her voice low and hoarse. 'Johnny.'

He probed for her name. 'And you?'

'I've seen you about,' she muttered.

'But you're not one of my patients.'

'I'm never ill,' she said, indicating by her tone that she couldn't allow herself to be.

Yet she looked ill. The strain was in the line of her neck and the wrinkles from her eyes. She had a strong line to her jaw, and a wide mouth, tight, with her lips thin. No colour on them. A practical young woman, in her late twenties, he guessed.

'You didn't say . . . ' He let it tail off gently, persuasively.

'Laura . . . ' She coughed and covered her mouth, but he knew she hadn't been about to say 'Parfitt'. The way she'd used his name. No wife would say that.

'You know him well? I mean, it could be helpful. Is he strong? Young?'

'Oh . . . strong!' She turned to face him at

last, loose chestnut hair flying from beneath a plastic rain hood. Her words tumbled out. 'You're not going to get him off there. I just know it. From what that man said. You're not!'

'They're not sure yet.' He tried again. 'You know him well?'

Then the passion went out of her voice, and she sounded dull and beaten. 'We were living together, at the farm, till they took him away. He's been in Parkhurst for four years. I didn't think . . . never imagined he'd want to come back to me. But he was, wasn't he? Coming back to me.' She ended it in stunned wonder.

So Grey had been wrong. Not just to evade the police. That hadn't been Johnny's sole reason for using the bridge, but to reach his woman as soon as possible.

'It seems he *was* coming to you, Laura. But it was rather unconventional transport. A wagon loaded with whisky.'

She was suddenly flustered. 'Whisky?' Her eyes wandered, disturbed by concentrated thought. Then she laughed abruptly, but there was no joy in it. 'Just like Johnny. The great idiot. It's just the sort of thing he'd do.'

'An expensive joyride,' he suggested.

'That's what he was, a lorry driver.'

It wasn't really an answer. They were silent.

He offered her a cigarette, but she shook her head. She seemed still to be deeply in thought. He waited. Then at last she spoke quietly.

'We had a little boy. Perhaps that was why Johnny was heading for the farm, probably thinking he's there.' Then, having tried to divert Johnny's motive from herself, she jerked away from the idea. 'No, that can't be right. He must know where Harry is. He'd be five now. Harry.'

Chris waited, scarcely breathing. He was unprepared for her wild entreaty.

'But you'll get him out of there. Please! Say you will.'

'We'll try our very best,' he said weakly.

'Say you will. Please. Promise me.'

He was reluctant with promises, aiming always to keep them. 'If it's up to me, of course.'

'You're the doctor.'

'For now. They could find someone better qualified.' Easily, he thought grimly.

Her eyes were swimming, moving as she examined his face. 'But it'll be you. Promise.'

'All right. I promise.' Or he'd have had another patient on his hands. 'I don't think you should stay, Laura. Nothing's going to happen for a long while.'

'You'll let me know? Troughton Farm.'

'I'll come and let you know.'

His reply seemed to have disconcerted her. 'No, not the farm. I have to stay. I'll be here.'

Now he was anxious to leave. Her intensity was disturbing him. She was close to hysteria, and he found himself struggling to consider her with the detachment he would have had for a patient.

'There's a conference,' he told her. 'I'll have to be there. I'll see you again, Laura.'

She nodded, smiling, her eyes bright. He slammed the door and walked away.

Moving along the road was a van with 'Midlands Television' on its side. It hadn't taken the media long to latch on to it. Their presence irritated him. He went to find the truck with the canvas cover, taking an armful of bottles from his car.

There were five people there already, sitting on oil drums round a hurricane lamp, with the rain pattering on the canvas and the wind flapping its corners. He pulled himself up with the rope.

Marson had it, and himself, in hand. The group sat round the lamp like a coven of witches, but to Marson it was as though he presided at the head of a conference table. Even in this setting he felt the comfort of his more natural ambience. At his right sat Jeff Fisher, his legs apart, head down, staring at his feet. To Jeff's right, the Fire Chief, still trying to be helpful. Grey was seated on Marson's left, rigid, somehow excited.

Chris said: 'I brought some beer.' Six bottles, he realised, as he put them down. Just right.

The sixth was Frank Allison. What he thought he was doing there Chris couldn't imagine, but he supposed it was in Frank's blood. He'd be protecting the community's interests, if any. Trust Frank.

'Good man,' said Grey, reaching for a bottle.

Chris found an oil drum. 'I just saw a TV van arriving,' he told them.

'Ghouls,' Marson said in disgust. 'They'll love it. They'll *want* to see that bridge crashing into the river.'

Chris shrugged. 'So disappoint them. Get him out of there . . . alive.'

'And that,' Marson said, looking round, 'is just what we're going to do. But they'll have to hang around quite a while for their pictures.'

Grey's head came up. He did not speak. Marson had their attention. He sat, knees together, his hands raised as though he was going to applaud. Those hands conducted a good part of his conversation, moving outwards, inwards, clasping and thumping his forehead. He plunged into what he knew best — theory.

'This is the position,' he said. 'You've all seen how things are. That bridge is in a critical condition, and we daren't risk another man on it. Not one. But we're going to get him out, and the doctor here is going to keep him alive for us until we do.' He looked at Chris. 'Aren't you?'

'If I can,' Chris said warily. 'His name's Johnny something, by the way.' He was terrible at remembering surnames.

Grey interrupted sharply. 'Where did you get that?'

'A woman called Laura. She knows him.'

'Then I'll have to see her — '

Marson's palms came together with a slap. 'His name's Johnny. Fine. But he'll die on our hands if we waste too much time. I can tell you now that his right foot's trapped.'

'We cut people out of wrecks like that every day — ' started the Fire Chief.

'No.' Marson was curt and to the point. 'Your machinery's too heavy. Even the plan to separate the cab from the trailer is too great a risk now. The only way to get him off the bridge is to lift the whole lorry clear. That — even if it is possible — will take time, and time is one thing that 'Johnny' doesn't have. The wind is not predictable enough to dangle anyone from the crane for any length of time. Suspended from only one point, there'd be no telling which way they'd be blown. But there is a way the doctor could reach him. We could run a cable across the river. The Kato would reach the other side. Jeff?'

Jeff looked up from his feet. He was not pleased with what he was hearing. 'We can reach to a hundred and fifty feet, with the fly-boom on.' His eyebrows were raised. He wondered whether Marson had had this in mind from the beginning.

Chris was starting to look pale.

'Right then,' continued Marson. 'That's settled. A cable across to the other cliff, alongside the wagon on its down-river side. The driver's window's missing and the cab's leaning out over the river. It shouldn't be too difficult. We anchor it the other side, and put a hand-winch on this end. We hook a chairlift on it with a couple of pulleys, so that we can tow it out and back. How's that sound, Chris? We could get you right to the cab window.'

It sounded terrible. The nightmare was with him again. 'So what do I do?' he demanded. 'Feel his pulse? Chuck him a sandwich?'

Marson didn't smile. 'Like a holiday in Switzerland, it'll be. Your own chairlift. You'll love it.'

'I'll dash home for my sunglasses,' he said, but his lips were sticking to his teeth.

Grey stirred uneasily. He couldn't understand the flippancy. But Marson still had their attention, and suddenly he was completely serious.

'There's something none of you knows. That cliff. I've had to survey it, you see. The new motorway bridge was due to come through here. I was fighting that, because I wanted to preserve Prescott's Bridge, but it's too late for that now. The point is that we'll never be able to take the motorway bridge over here to replace it. I wasn't sure about it before. Now I'm dead certain. That cliff is what we call argillaceous rock, on both sides of the river. That sort of rock's formed from clays and silts, millions of years back. So this is compacted shale, and the stuff's notorious for its tendency to suffer plastic deformation. That means that there's lamination parallel with the bedding planes, and they're a bit prone to failure by flow. Especially when wet. I'm simplifying this a bit, but the weight of the bridge and the wagon, combined with the sudden extra load and the weather, are bringing the cliffs down. And as the bedding planes are vertical, and in line with the river, they'll come down in great sodding slabs from a point just behind the support piles for Prescott's chains.'

It had all been said with the quiet authority of absolute conviction. Not one voice was raised in dispute. No one spoke for some moments; it was a large concept to assimilate. Eventually, it was Frank Allison who spoke.

'You mean . . . ' He was still feeling for it. 'You mean, into our river?'

Marson turned to face him. He did not know who Allison was, and didn't appreciate the fire in his eyes. He took it for a trick of the light. 'Exactly, sir.'

'But it'd block the narrows. The valley, the whole valley . . . '

'Would be flooded,' Marson completed for him calmly. Having heard Johnny scream, his course was fixed. 'If we were to go out there now and drop the bridge and the wagon, the river would probably not hesitate for a second. But lose the cliffs . . . ' He pursed his lips, and his palms came together again. His voice became rough. 'A bit like hanging, isn't it? It's easy to argue that you'd like vicious murderers to be hanged, for the good of the community. But *you* don't have to pull the lever. And so, for the welfare of this community, we could cut it all loose, while the cliffs are still standing. But who's going to use the cutter on the chains?' His eyes were on Allison, whom he'd at last typed.

'This is completely academic,' Allison protested uneasily.

'There might be another way,' Marson said, 'a way not to make that choice at all, not even academically. We might be able to support the whole bridge, wagon, the lot.'

Jeff's head came up, and he blinked.

Marson reached to his feet for his bottle, put it to his lips, then peered past it. 'There'll be little time. The cliffs are already sliding.'

'So what d'you want to *do*?' Grey growled.

'We throw cables across the river. Two-inch steel cables. How are we, Jeff?'

'Three lengths,' Jeff muttered, not happy with the fancy plans he was hearing.

'Good. We throw two across, supported well above the bridge on tripods, further apart than the chains, use the other in two lengths as slings under the bridge, and take the weight off the chains. And then . . . ' He jutted his lower lip, his hands stretched out each side of his face. 'Then the cliffs will be safe, and we can take our time picking the whole wagon off.'

There was silence as they avoided each other's eyes. To Chris it didn't sound too good. Take their time, Marson had said, picking off the wagon. But was there time for Johnny? Jeff was wondering what hell the boss

68

back at headquarters would raise when he heard of all this. Allison was bewildered. It was Grey who cleared his throat.

'How long will all this take?' he asked.

'For the cable over the river for the doctor's chairlift — say a couple of hours. For the main cables to support the bridge . . . what d'you say, Jeff? A day? Maybe more?'

Jeff looked embarrassed to have the decision thrust at him. 'Without details of how you're thinking . . . ' He was shaking his head. It was not certain they'd be allowed to spend so long at the bridge; company property, company men.

'There must be a quicker way,' started Chris.

'No.' Marson was cold. 'Several cranes are big enough to bear the weight of that trailer, but most are too big. Put a five-hundred tonner on those cliffs and the whole lot will come straight down. We could never get one into either of the cutaways — they're much too narrow. The only crane that can do it — the only crane to which we have access — is the Jones. And, as Jeff can tell you, the Jones will take time.'

Frank Allison felt the weight himself, the agonising responsibility of deciding his point of view. One life weighed against the appalling consequences if the plan failed and the cliffs fell. 'We'll have to give it a try,' he said softly. Then he looked down at his feet.

Poor Frank, thought Chris fondly. For so long he'd argued the claim of the district's minority against the greater gain of the majority. Now he was still representing the same people, the community, but it had suddenly become the majority. Nobody could represent Johnny. He was the smallest minority you could get. And he'd got no say in the matter, nothing but that single scream. The final irony was that the same circumstances had brought about Frank's triumph for the community against the motorway. Whatever happened, the concrete bridge would not cross the river just there.

'Good,' said Marson, rolling the empty bottle between his palms. 'Then we'll need a few things. Such as mains water, electricity laid on — we'll have to have proper floodlights on the cliff — and a phone to my caravan . . . '

'I'll do what I can,' mumbled Grey. He spoke as though there was something on his mind.

' . . . by morning. There're things I've got to get moving. Jeff, you'd better send Cropper back with this truck, when we've finished in here. We'll need the full team.'

'Sievewright'll go mad,' said Jeff.

Marson tapped his knee. 'Jeff, I've been eight years at head office. I can handle him. Get the lot over here. All the caravans. The Land-rover had better stay where it is, at the top of the cliffs.'

'There are details we've got to discuss,' said Jeff, his voice tight.

'I know, and we will.'

'I'm not sure we can handle all this. And we've only got one eighty-ton crane.'

Then Marson's voice cracked out, the tension finally reacting to the opposition. 'For Christ's sake do it, and don't argue. I've already had the pants scared off me.'

But Jeff was calm. 'That chairlift alone'll be no picnic.'

Marson stared at him, then turned to Chris. 'We're going to look after you, Chris. We're going to rig you a chairlift so safe you could dance on it.'

'Dance on it, yes,' said Chris. 'But not much else, from what I can gather. Do you really expect me to work through the side window? That's what it sounded like to me. A lot I can do like that, I must say.'

'More than you could do by standing on the cliff and looking at it.' Marson's tone was beginning to betray something cold, a distant determination.

Chris stood up, rolled the oil drum away,

and stretched. His head touched the canvas roof, and he had to bend his neck. He shrugged. 'Three hours, did you say? I'll be back.'

Then he climbed down and returned along the road, but the Mini had gone. He didn't know the location of Troughton Farm, and in any event the woman had made it clear that she didn't want him there. She would have to wait to discover what splendid plans they had for her Johnny.

The whole mish-mash of the scheme sounded to Chris like wild fantasy. Because he couldn't visualise it as reality, it had seemed quite reasonable to promise he'd be back.

6

The sudden and spectacular return of Johnny into her life had completely confused Laura. She was not a woman with a flexible mind; new ideas required careful treatment, or they would skitter away before she could resolve them.

There was Den, that was the trouble, Den always in the background, there when she looked round, gone again the moment she turned back. Den used the farm as a convenience, but Johnny . . .

Johnny had come first, to the farm to live, to help her old dad with the milking. But Johnny had never really taken to farm work. He'd always been a driver, and it was Laura who eventually persuaded him to return to it. He did not have to leave. He remained at the farm, but spent a large part of his life on the road. Behind a wheel he was always happy.

Johnny had introduced her to Den in a pub, one of his mates, and very soon Den got to coming to the farm when Johnny was away, to cheer up her dad, he said. Den could be great fun, telling his stories. He could do all the voices, standing there in the living-room with his legs apart, ducking his head. He'd have her father nearly out of his chair, laughing. Den was good at that. It was only later, when it was too late, that Laura found he had another side to him. One second a smile, then something crazy — anything. And the harm he could do. Like a mad dog, he'd seem, raging and vicious. But way behind it, wild or not, Den was always in control.

That was what really terrified Laura. It was only gradually that she got to know he was a crook. Nothing grand. Hijacking. Small stuff. Talk to him and you'd think he was a master criminal, but it was nothing bigger than small vans — until he got Johnny involved with it. Then it was a wagon loaded with whisky.

Poor Johnny was a pushover for Den, who could twirl him around a finger. Hold up that finger, and Johnny would bark. Eventually, they planned something together. At least, Johnny thought it was together. It was his own load that was involved this time. He was going to let Den hijack it from him, Den and one other chap to drive it away, Johnny's wagon, and Den was going to tap Johnny on the head to make it look good. Johnny said he didn't want it to be his own wagon, but Den soon persuaded him. Of course, things went wrong. Laura was never sure exactly what, as she couldn't face going to Johnny's trial. All she knew was that a policeman was killed in a police car, and Johnny was the only one they could put their hands on, so he paid for the lot.

Now Johnny was coming home to her, when she thought he'd never come near again, not with Den virtually taking over the farm. Even before that hijack, Den had been using the empty barns to dump his hauls in. It seemed natural for Den to hide out at the farm, and Johnny must've known that, because he got a note out to him. Laura never found out what was in that note, but it was the first taste she got of Den's viciousness. The effect had lasted for months; perhaps it lingered even now. But Johnny *had* come back. Or at least had tried.

And there he was on the bridge, so that all of a sudden she was all mixed up, and she didn't know what to think. The last thing she wanted when she got home was for Den to be waiting up for her. She needed some time to herself.

At first she thought the light at the farm was her dad getting up to milk the cows. It was getting on for that time. The farm was three miles by road from the river, across the valley, and backing on to the pine-strewn slope behind. She could detect the pin point of light a mile away, and could watch it all the way up the long, muddy drive. The Mini was good in mud. But when she parked it by the old pump in the yard she knew it wasn't her father. He'd have had the door open and be asking, was that you, Laura? The old fuss-pot, she thought fondly. But the door remained shut.

So she walked in there, knowing it was to face Den. He wasn't going to be happy about Johnny being on the bridge, and she wasn't sure how to tell him.

'Where you been?' he asked in his emotionless voice. He hadn't been worrying for her, she thought, you can bet.

She told him she'd been at the bridge. 'Prescott's Bridge. The one with the chains.'

'It's after four!' he shouted, doing his outraged husband act, though she'd have died before marry him.

She had been hanging her coat up. It was soaked. She would have liked to get her clothes off, and into a dressing gown, but instead she said she would get some tea, saying it casually, as though the bridge was not suddenly the focus of her life. It kept her busy, her eyes occupied, while she told him. He had known she was going to visit her friend Cora on the other side of the river, to see the new baby, and that she would have used that bridge.

'But I couldn't get back across,' she told him. 'It was blocked by a great trailer wagon. I had to go all the way round to the town bridge, and then . . . well, I had to go and see what it was all about.'

'Stupid, nosy women,' he said, but it hadn't really registered because he was only grumbling.

'I thought it could be you,' she told him, though she hadn't thought that for a second. It wasn't in his league, a wagon-load of whisky that size. 'Thought you'd been heading back here with your latest wonderful whisky hijack.'

'Whisky?' It was that word which caught his attention. 'A wagon-load of scotch?'

'Oh, huge,' she said. 'I thought you'd moved into the big time. But it wasn't you, was it? And you haven't.'

He hooked his fingers into her arm, and he knew he was hurting her. 'Then who was it, you stupid bitch?'

'You ought to be pleased,' she said, trying to smile. She managed to get her arm free, but she could feel his eyes on her as she moved away. 'I've been keeping the best bit till the end.' She turned to face him, hoping she had some imitation of delight on her face. 'It was Johnny, Den. Just out of prison, and bringing you a present. A wagon-load of scotch, and all for you.'

That did it. The teapot went across the room, the cups after it, and he was raving. 'You stupid, bloody bitch. Don't you ever see anything? They'll trace him here. They'll know he was bringing it somewhere, and they'll search around. They want me, and they'll come here . . . when he tells 'em . . . '

'But you needn't *be* here, Den,' she said quietly.

She had been wanting to say something like that for ages, though in a more direct way. Something like: 'Sod off, Den, we don't want you.' But she hadn't dared. This was as close as she'd ever come to it, and her heart was hammering. He was looking at her with his head sideways, considering her. He had his twisted smile on his face. It went on for ages. Her legs felt weak, and she could have screamed.

'You don't mean that, Laura,' he said at last, shaking his head, sad for her. 'Oh, you'd like to see the back of me, I'm sure, but it suits me here. It's gonna take something special to shift me, and it ain't gonna come from you.'

But he was sounding quite reasonable for a change. She jumped right in, taking her chance.

'But Johnny's there, Den. There on the

bridge. He was coming back to me — and you didn't expect that, did you?' She was sticking her neck right out, shouting it at him almost in triumph. 'And Johnny knows where his parents took my Harry. You and Johnny know where. So now you can go, Den. Bugger off, for all I care. I've got Johnny . . . '

But she hadn't. Not got him, by any means, and she knew it. So when she'd finished that bit she was shaking, and Den knew it'd been all bluff. He had an instinct for that sort of thing. In a second he was at her, both hands clawing at her arms. He banged her down on a chair, standing over her, then with one hand he grabbed her chin, so that she couldn't help but look at him, and his other fist hovering on the edge of her sight was an emphatic threat. Her shadow of advantage had gone. She didn't dare to take it any further because Johnny was still far from her, and there wasn't any way he was going to be able to tell her where they'd got her Harry.

In effect, it all came down to Harry. He'd been a baby — not much more — when Den came to the farm, but it wasn't very long before she realised she didn't want Harry anywhere near Den. It seemed as though Den couldn't stand the sight of him, probably because he was Johnny's, and Johnny wasn't around any more. She was frightened for her child. So when Johnny was sent down, she asked Johnny's parents to take Harry for a while. They were only too happy to have him. They would have taken Laura, too, but she couldn't leave her dad alone on the farm with Den. The Parfitts seemed to understand at first. They kept in touch, sent her photographs; sometimes she heard Harry over the phone. But after the first year, things weren't the same. Their letters became shorter. They were less about Harry and more about Johnny. Once or twice, they even mentioned Den. After a while, she hadn't heard from them for over a month. Then one of her letters came back marked 'not known at this address'.

Laura thought she understood what had happened. They had decided she wasn't a fit person to have charge of their son's child. That could be just the way they'd think about it, her living with Den, that sort of thing. Den said that he knew where the Parfitts had gone, that he knew people who knew, but he wouldn't tell her, not until he was ready. She was in no position to doubt him — she had too little else. But one thing was certain: if Den ever contacted the Parfitts, he would certainly not have told them that Laura would not have him near her bedroom.

At that time she knew she would never get

rid of him. With Johnny turned against her by his parents — or so she imagined — she might never see Harry again, which made her absolutely dependent on Den. And Den never revealed a thing, leering at her, using it to bolster his demands. If not for that, she would have killed him. Yes, she really thought she would.

But he knew his hold on her was as strong as ever. She'd made the mistake of faltering, right at the end, and he pounced on it.

'Now you're gonna tell me,' he said. 'The truth. Johnny comin' to you! Load of rubbish. He was coming to me, with that blasted whisky. To me. Here. But we don't want the police here. If they'd got to him, they'd be here right now. So out with it! Come on!'

There wasn't any point in not telling him. He could go and look for himself.

'He's stuck on the bridge.' She had to shake her chin free. 'They don't know if they can get to him. They don't know if they can get him off, and if they do, he could be dead.' As she was saying it, she felt a deep, sad loss, like something dragging out of her. But the loss was Harry. And for Johnny . . . oh God, she couldn't feel anything.

'Hah!' Den was pleased with that, his tone making her flesh crawl, but the way he pranced about the room meant his nerves were on edge. It was all too close to him, even though the police couldn't know how close. 'So you'd better pray, Laura. Pray good and hard that Johnny dies.'

She was horrified. 'I can't do that.' She stared at him. 'That's terrible. You shouldn't even say such a wicked thing . . . '

''Cause if he don't, if he seems like saying one bloody word to anybody, then I'll have to do something about it.'

Even then she didn't understand what he meant. She was still trying to sort out exactly what he had in mind when her father wandered into the room, scratching his head and saying:

'Ain't you two been to bed?'

7

Chris realised that there was no point in trying to get a couple of hours' sleep. He went home only because he didn't want to watch what they were rigging for him, on the same principle as going missing while the plumber repairs a burst water-pipe. He ran a bath and got something to eat, and sprayed the kitchen with deodorant, then left the cat asleep on the top of the fridge while he went to have a look at the river, no farther away than the bottom end of the street.

It was still raining. The water was a noisy surge, almost at his toes, not visible apart from catches of light on its broken surface. The menacing suck and grumble of it drove him away. Looking down-river he could see the concentration of light where they were working on the cliffs, with odd little spurts of blue flame that he couldn't identify.

It seemed to him that Marson could well be wrong when he said the falling bridge and wagon would have little effect on the river. The water seemed to be backing and thrusting as it narrowed for the pass between the cliffs. It didn't seem that it could absorb any further opposition.

He picked up a blanket and some more equipment from his surgery and drove back to the bridge. Laura worried him. She'd left a number of unanswered questions in his mind, and he'd promised to look her up again — as of course he would have to. She was nowhere to be seen when he got back to the activity on the cliffs. No sign of her car. It was still completely dark. It might have been six o'clock, but time didn't seem to have any relevance. He walked up the slope to the concentration of light, which was on the eastern cliff, and there found Frank Allison, wet, cold and untidy, and his usual pig-headed self.

'You're not supposed to look at the flashes,' Allison told him, having used his usual methods of nosing out what was afoot. 'It's the ultra-violet, or something.'

The blue flashes Chris had seen were the welding strikes where they were putting together the sturdy tripods to support Marson's main cables, which were to come later. They had a portable generator throbbing away.

'Go home, Frank,' he tried.

'No.' He drew closer, nudging Chris's shoulder. 'I've seen the cracks.'

Chis surveyed the top of the cliffs. It was

serrated with a whole surface of indentations, in line with the river. 'It's nothing but cracks, Frank.'

'You can shine a torch down some of them,' Allison said tensely. 'I've done it. Chris, d'you think he knows what he's doing?'

Just as he was about to answer, Chris had just noticed what Marson was preparing for him. His throat was suddenly tight. He thumped Allison on the shoulder to cover his feelings. 'Of course he does,' he said. 'He's a civil engineer. All the qualifications.'

But he was asking himself what those might be. What looked like a line of thread disappeared into the far shadows, and dropped across in a shallow loop. This end, it began to look like a clothes line, and at his feet it became a half-inch cable. They had brought it fifty feet back from the edge, and wrapped it round the drum of a hand winch, which they'd pegged to the rock. Nobody was near the handle. A small, minor and puny comma of metal was locked into the ratchet. Chris went forward, drawn by the horror of it. Marson was standing with his feet apart near the edge, a loudhailer in his hand, and was belting out instructions across the river. A pinpoint of light answered with a double wink.

'Does that mean we're ready?' asked Grey,

who was standing at his shoulder. 'Where the hell's that bloody doctor?'

'He's here,' Chris said, his voice hard, looking for an excuse to walk away.

Marson turned. His smile was a little strained. 'Ah, there you are,' he said brightly. 'We've had a bit of luck.' He gestured. 'The wind's dropped,' he explained, because there wasn't anything lucky that Chris could see.

The bridge was barely moving. From the cliff top there was little noise, just the odd shudder and whine. The skin was tight over Chris's face.

They had used the same four-by-one plank, the same ropes, the only difference being that they had hooked them over a pulley on the cable, and had a nylon rope from the pulley, both ways across the river. This end, three men were hanging on to it. He could only hope that an equal number were over there in the pitch black emptiness he was due to head for.

'I'm glad about the wind,' Chris said. 'Would somebody please explain what I'm supposed to do?'

He was expected to sit on it, that was what. Sit passively, while they hauled him to and fro, and lifted or lowered the cable with the hand winch, thus holding him in reasonable proximity to his objective — that broken window on the driver's side.

Sensing his lack of enthusiasm, Marson said: 'We'll rig it better, later on, so that we can operate it entirely from this side.'

Later on! Chris felt a nerve jerk in his cheek. There was nothing he could get at, nothing he could stick a fist into or put a shoulder to. And to what end? For one second his anger at its futility overrode everything else.

'You're damned crazy!' he said angrily. 'What can I do from that thing? How can I get at the poor bastard, for Christ's sake?'

Marson looked shocked. He'd been so proud of it. 'It's the best ... in the circumstances ... '

'No!' Chris shot out his hands, dismissing it. 'The whole thing's ridiculous.'

'But you could try, Chris. Give it a try, huh?'

It was so unlike Marson that it caught Chris at a disadvantage. Not once had he heard an appeal from Marson, but now he looked whipped, and somehow it became Chris who was being ridiculous with his protests. So what alternative did that leave him?

He hefted his bag. 'Do you swear to me that your cable will stand up?'

'It'd take a bus,' Marson said, suddenly

confident again. 'Now look, you just sit on it, sideways, bag beside you. I'll be here with the loudhailer. I'll watch every move. Do exactly what I tell you — exactly. And Chris — this is damned important — don't put any weight on the vehicle. Not one bit of weight.'

Talking steadily, keeping Chris's mind off it, he got him seated on the chairlift, his feet still dragging on the cliff surface. Chris was aware of a rumble of comment, and realised that a fair contingent of locals had gathered just behind the group of coppers, who were supposed to be keeping them back. He searched for a face in the shadows, and they shot him out over the river.

He had wanted to prepare himself, or something like that; at least manage to wave to the TV cameras. There wasn't time. He plunged. The board swung and twisted beneath him. It caught his breath, or he might have shouted out.

The vehicle seemed endless yards down. Chris was certain he was about to plunge into the river. Its roar reached for him, and he was jolted to a halt. He sat swaying and clearing his eyes of rain, and there before him, and above him because it was leaning right over the chair, was the driver's side of the towing unit. He was too low. His heart was pounding. He clutched a rope, and waited.

The steel platform of the bridge protruded a foot beyond the points where the hanger bars had been fixed. Most of them had snapped off in that stretch of the bridge, some short, some longer. The huge driving wheels were pressed out beyond the hanger stubs, and seemed to be flexing, back and forth, only a couple of inches from the ultimate edge. He stared at the cab door. There was just himself and the cab. That seemed to help. The door was buckled but unbroken, though just in front the body was pierced by what appeared to be a piece from the parapet. It had snapped off just on the outside. He looked at it a long while before the significance penetrated his brain. It was at the point where the foot pedals would be.

All this time the loudhailer was blaring across the river. If any of the instructions were for Chris, he certainly didn't hear them. The chair swayed and began to lift. The shattered window lowered itself to his eyes. The edges of broken glass were jagged. As there seemed to be nothing he could do sitting there, he stood up, sliding his left hand up the rope.

The lean of the cab fooled him. Sitting, he'd been well clear of it. Standing, he could almost lean against it — or it against him. The broken rim of glass along the door-sill was opposite his stomach. He was swaying. The board was insecure beneath his feet. He just had to find some support, and gripped the vertical edge of the window with his right hand. Then he did what he could.

'Johnny,' he called, 'I'm a doctor. Can you hear me?'

There was no answer, or if there was he lost it in all that groaning of metal and the roar of the river. He was cold, and almost in despair. He had never felt so useless. Almost in anger, he hooked the fingers of his left hand in the door handle. The loudhailer was clattering away, out near the middle of the bridge the noise was intense. He stopped trying to hear, and concentrated. He reached inside with his right shoulder, then his head. By straining his back and leg muscles, he managed to put no weight on anything but the door handle.

There was a little light. Johnny's head was very low and to Chris's left. He groped, touching flesh. It was cool and moist. He tried for the jugular, and found it. Faint and slow heartbeat. Shock? Exposure? He snatched at the blanket by his side and forced it in through the window, clumsily covering Johnny's chest. He felt helpless, and terribly, horribly aware of that shattered steel through the side of the cab. Morphine? It was completely unprofessional, when he couldn't even check the respiration. But he'd have to have it.

'Johnny! Can you hear me?'

There was not a movement beneath his fingers. If Johnny had been conscious, Chris might have got him to take down a couple of tablets. But now it'd have to be by syringe. And how the hell was he going to do that with one hand?

He had always considered that he did a reasonable job as a doctor, but this was outside all reason. He was hashing it, he knew, being too aware of his own danger, rushing and fumbling, and cursing himself because he was falling short of his own standards.

On his knees on the board, he managed to get the bag open, broke a pack of ampoules, tore the cover from a sterilised syringe. God, that was hygenic, with the rainwater streaming from his chin onto his hands! He gave it half a grain, poised the syringe, and heaved himself to his feet again. The chair plunged, and he waited, barely breathing, for it to settle. His knees were shaking. He straightened, high on his toes, leg muscles on fire. The blasted board beneath his feet wouldn't stay still.

He had to get both elbows inside. The shards of glass were painful beneath his arms.

Left shoulder low, he reached for a wrist. There had to be a wrist, for heaven's sake. He found it. Both shoulders were inside now. He was trying for intravenous. The vein came up. He was dully aware of the loudhailer, forcing itself into the edges of his consciousness. There was no time for finesse. Needle in, plunger down, slowly and steadily . . . straight into the vein . . .

Johnny groaned and stirred. 'You're all right, Johnny,' Chris said. 'It's not going to hurt any more.'

That was a prayer, for both of them. He tossed the syringe aside. He found he couldn't see or feel the board at all by that time, and he had to kick for it, wriggling himself out, toes reaching for the bag, fearful of pushing it over the side.

The loudhailer cracked out at him: 'Get down out of there, you damned fool!'

He blinked down for the board, blinded by sweat and rain. His hands were on the shards of glass, but he couldn't feel anything. He contacted the bag with his toe, allowed himself to slip down a couple of inches, then had a foot down, both feet, and slowly, shaking with exhaustion and sheer, bloody terror, he crouched down, one foot each side of the bag, his head lowered, and sick with the swing of the chair.

For a while he fumbled to open the bag. His hands seemed useless. It was necessary to keep telling himself that he'd got to get antibiotic into Johnny. But he couldn't make any definite or positive movement towards accomplishing it, or even concentrate on what was required.

'We're bringing you in.'

He realised it had been blasting at him for some time, and raised his head. There was nothing but a glare of light, like a whole fleet of cars roaring down on him. He tried to shout: No! Give me two minutes, he wanted to cry out. Give me time to get my nerve back.

But he didn't get time. Suddenly the chair fell beneath him as though the cable had snapped. He remembered thinking that the bastard had promised him it would take a bus, then he was plunging down towards the water.

8

Marson knew there was nothing wrong with the chairlift. In the time they'd had, it was something of an achievement. Not his. Jeff had supervised it, using two teams of half a dozen men in each.

They had used the Kato with its fly-boom on to ferry them across, and to send over the end of the half-inch cable. Marson went across with his foot in the hook, like the others, and after the episode on the bridge it had seemed quite tame. He wanted to show them where to anchor the cable and where to locate the tripod, but Jeff didn't seem in a good mood. Impatient with him, somehow. So Marson had left them to it, though watching hadn't done his nerves any good at all.

By that time they'd brought most of the caravans along, and the rest of their equipment was on its way. Peterson had got the mobile kitchen going, so Marson went along for a cup of tea, thinking he might have a boosting chat with some of the chaps who were there, but they weren't responsive, and soon drifted away.

Marson had been eight years at head office, feeding figures into the computer and running off photocopies of bridge designs. He'd been bored with it, and getting nowhere. As Sievewright said, in one of his rare mellow moods, Marson was heading up a blind alley. He needed field experience. So when a JCB rolled onto Big Jim Corrigan and killed him, Marson applied for the job, and got it. He was the only applicant. Everybody else knew you couldn't pick up with Big Jim's team, everybody except Marson.

Big Jim was a legend. They said he'd wander round in circles, stop, dig his heel in the ground, and there they'd find bedrock for a pile. They said he could find a roadway across a swamp in the dead of night. His men had worshipped him. Marson, with his soundings and his calculations, could also find the same bedrock. But Big Jim did it in minutes; it took Marson days.

They didn't trust Marson, and he couldn't get near them. He was the theory boy, and apparently they couldn't even bring themselves to drink tea with him. They drifted away. He went to find where they'd put his caravan, and tried to dry out. But he hadn't been doing the job long enough, so hadn't got all the waterproofs he really needed. A cup of coffee, a few biscuits, then he headed back to the cliff, still wet and not feeling too good.

The trouble was that he'd tried to do what Big Jim would've done: make instant decisions. There, in the back of the truck, he'd produced a scheme that he'd hardly had time to consider properly. It'd sounded good. 'This is what we'll do, and it'll work.' Yet there were so many imponderables: how high for the main tripods, how far apart, what lengths of cable for the support slings? None of these details had been computed, and yet already a start had been made on the main tripods. Now he was aching to get at his paperwork and calculator, to lay out his force projections, and prove to himself that it had a possibility of working.

The chairlift was no more than an elementary exercise. The two teams had been rehearsed, three men each side of the river with control ropes. Cropper had charge of the winch. Marson had simply omitted to tell him to remain by it, and not take his great fist off the handle. But once they had the chairlift at the correct height, and the ratchet pawl home, there wasn't really any more for Cropper to do. Natural curiosity lured him to Marson's elbow. Marson didn't notice him there, being too concentrated on that stubborn idiot Chris Keene and what he was doing at the bridge. At one stage it seemed that he was going to climb right inside the cab.

Marson went wild with the loudhailer, but as far as he could tell, Chris wasn't hearing. Then, when he finally crouched down on the plank they'd rigged for him, Marson was sure he'd finished. He called out that they were bringing him in. Chris simply squatted, not lifting his head, and for a moment Marson was worried that he was hurt. Then, just as he was going to give the order to haul him in, abruptly he fell away as though the cable had broken. At the same time Marson heard a snap, which it took him a split-second to identify as coming from the winch. He whirled round, but it was ten yards away. He could do nothing but shout out frantically.

But Cropper was already moving. He was a bulky man, with a chubby, vacant face that gave the impression of stupidity. In one dive he was scattering the group of public gawpers, and Marson saw then the rapidly rotating handle of the winch. It was not much more than a blur, and he wouldn't have dared put a limb near it. But Cropper threw himself on it, then he was grappling with both hands, and holding it. He got to his knees, his head hanging for one second. He stared back at Marson.

Marson looked for Chris, and he could see

nothing of him. He'd fallen way down beneath the concentration of light. All they could do was pray that he was there. Marson turned back to Cropper.

'Wind him up!' he shouted.

Cropper got to his feet and wound stolidly with one hand. His other arm hung slack, and his face was expressionless. Marson was shouting for a torch. There was one in the Land-rover they'd brought up, but there wasn't time. He stared down. The cable creaked tautly, and slowly, into the shadows and then into the light, the chairlift came up.

Chris was hanging face down across it, one arm over the side, and ridiculously dangling the medical bag in his fingers. They brought him in slowly and gently. Marson wouldn't let Cropper leave the winch, even when he'd got the cable taut. He heard the ratchet pawl locked in again.

Jeff and Marson hauled Chris off the board. He wasn't unconscious, just hanging with his mouth open, gasping on the edge of terror. They sat him on the cliff top. Blood was running from his hands. Cropper stood with his legs apart, staring.

Chris levered himself to his feet, like a rugby player who'd been pounded into the mud. His breathing was still bad. They could barely understand him.

'What happened?' he managed to get out. 'I wanted to . . . '

'The ratchet slipped. Cropper got to the handle.'

Chris looked at Cropper, but he was talking to Marson. 'I wanted to get some antibiotic . . . into him. It's not finished. I'll have to go back.'

'No.' Marson wasn't having that. 'The ratchet's faulty. Later, perhaps.' He was having to be firm. Chris had a startled look of incomprehension about him. Besides, he looked dangerous. 'We'll re-rig it. Safer. You'll see. But later.'

Jeff had a hand round Chris's shoulders. Chris was trying to throw him off.

'He's half unconscious,' he was stammering. 'Shock. Exposure. God knows what else. I can't do anything — *anything* — through that sodding window.' He was close to sobbing, Marson saw. 'You've got to get me to him, for Christ's sake. I'll have to get a drip . . . have to . . . '

Then it all tailed away, with him shaking his head and groaning, and he just started walking. Allison reached out to pat his shoulder, but Chris didn't even see him. People stood aside, whispering, and he moved through them as though he was blind, until he stood in front of Cropper. He stared at his hands, shook his head, then muttered: 'Thanks. I'll see you . . . ' Then he moved on, and a woman ran out of the darkness and took his arm. They went away together.

Grey had come to life, aware of the growing crowd of sightseers. With growls and oaths he got his men moving, and the area was cleared rapidly. Jeff was at Marson's elbow, Cropper still at his winch. Marson spoke to him.

'Want a word with you, Cropper. Why the hell did you leave the damned thing?' He believed he was speaking calmly, but his nerves were on edge and it came out as a snarl.

Cropper jerked his head. 'It seemed safe.' His voice had no intonation in it. 'I wanted to watch.'

Jeff put in: 'Hold on. What's that on the ground? Look.' He was gesturing with his toe.

Somebody had found the torch. It shone on a crowbar they'd used for the rigging. It lay now beside the winch. Marson dropped to one knee.

'You think . . . ?'

Slowly, Allison and Grey became aware of the interest and joined the group. Grey crouched beside Marson. 'Could it have been deliberate?' he asked quietly.

Cropper was still there. 'Ratchet pawls

don't just jump out. But one bang with that thing . . . '

'Oh no,' said Marson quickly. It was something beyond his imagination.

Allison got to his feet. He was solemn and ponderous. 'There's a mood,' he said. 'I've been moving around, listening. There's real fear in the air. You can almost smell it. This bridge, sitting here, it's a threat. A . . . a person could want it down, before it takes the cliffs with it.'

'I can't believe that,' Marson replied, unconvincingly.

'If your whole life was in a farm down on the low ground, it'd seem very valid.' Grey nodded, pressing it home. 'Not everybody thinks logically. And of course it may not be so. But just in case it is, I'll tighten things up around here. And you'd better get things moving, whatever it is you've got in mind. Let 'em see something happening.'

He'd got Marson's mind whirling and for a few moments he couldn't concentrate. What *was* there to do? Then Jeff brought him back.

'Cropper's finished one of the main tripods,' he said. 'Done a good job.'

Marson went with him to have a look at it. These things had to be strong, as they were going to take the whole weight — bridge, wagon, the lot — two each side of the river.

This one was fine, but Marson, unable to prevent himself from worrying about Chris, failed to compliment Cropper.

'Jeff,' he said, 'why not throw a transceiver into the cab. Tune it to the radio in the Land-rover, then we can hear him if he speaks.'

Jeff said, voice clipped: 'I'll do it, Colin. Later. We've got to get on, though. The other crane . . . '

Marson forced his mind to it. The idea was to put a strong tripod, eight feet tall, on the peaks of the two cliffs each side of the river. They would use the two-inch cable over them, and anchor it into the rock, well back, using two diesel-powered winches this side. Then they would rig slings under the bridge and wind in the main cables, and . . . the Jones.

The Jones was a different crane altogether from the Kato. It had a rigid, latticed boom, which had to be rigged — or stripped down — manually; it ran on tracks instead of wheels, like a huge, lumbersome tank, and had a maximum mobile speed of five miles an hour. Above all, the Kato was *their* equipment; but the Jones was the main lifting tackle at the construction site, twenty miles behind them. And whereas the advance team could afford to lose a day or two, and pull it back, the main team was on a tight schedule, with crippling penalty clauses in the contract. Jeff might not have understood the implications as Marson did. The main team could not afford to release the Jones.

' . . . let's go and start it moving,' Jeff said with quiet enthusiasm. Still Marson hesitated. But he could do nothing to overcome the main team's obstructions until he knew what those obstructions would be. 'Let's do that,' he agreed, and he moved away, leaving Jeff to fall into step.

They had brought in the radio wagon along with the rest. The complete outfit was assembled in a scattered circle on the flat ground over by the line of trees. Like a circus. The light was just coming into the sky, sluggish, though there was a hopeful line of clear orange over in the east. It caught the bright blue and yellow motif of the Sevco vehicles.

Jeff was talking anxiously as they walked. 'How're we going to anchor the main cables each side?'

Marson shrugged impatiently. 'I thought we'd dig channels. Say ten feet by four by four. Over the other side we'll have a girder welded to each cable and buried in concrete. This side, two diesel winches bolted onto the concrete beds. Better get the compressor up and the pneumatic drills going.'

'We can't do that.' Jeff was emphatic. 'Not pneumatic drills on that rock. The vibration'd have it down.'

'Then how?'

'I'll get Charlie Maine to blast 'em out.'

'Explosives? That'd be crazy.'

Jeff was shaking his head. 'Little blasts. A lot of 'em. Charlie can do it. I've seen him lift a single brick from a wall.'

After a second, Marson nodded, and they continued walking. 'Anything else?'

'We're a bit short of high-alumina cement.'

The stuff was rarely used in high-quality work. But it was fast setting, and speed was what they needed.

'How short?'

'It'll be a sixty-forty mix.'

'That'll have to do.'

'It'll slow down the setting.'

'Then you'll have to get the channels dug that much quicker. This Charlie Maine of yours . . . ' Marson shrugged, and let it ride. They plodded along side by side.

'And we're not too well off for two-inch cable,' Jeff said at last. He sounded mournful, but Marson could have sworn Jeff was enjoying it.

'For God's sake. What've we got?'

'Three lengths; eighty metres each.'

Marson did it in his head. One length cut in half for the slings. That left the two main support cables, each 80 metres — only 250 feet. With 135 feet of river to span, they would have little to spare each side. Take away waste in the sag, in the peaks over the tripods, in the take-up for the winches, and the anchors would be only 45 feet from the cliff edges. It was not enough, Marson felt, not with that cliff.

He groaned, but kept moving. His mind was racing. Stresses, angles, pressures. 'Then we'll have to make the channels twenty feet long,' he decided. He glanced at Jeff. 'Twice as long, but just as soon, Jeff. There might not be much time.'

Jeff grunted. 'Bigger channels, slower setting.'

Marson shouldered open the door into the radio shack. Ray Foster lived there. He kept the walkie-talkies working, and operated the radio that kept them in touch with the main team. He would supply a transceiver for the wagon's cab, when they were ready for it.

He was asleep in the bunk beside his bench, asleep in his old set of dungarees, but was awake in an instant. His mongrel growled warningly in his ear. Foster was going on sixty, and he looked undressed without his headphones. Jeff told him that Mr Marson wanted to speak to the main team, which wasn't quite true. Marson really wanted to talk to Sievewright at head office first — it was ultimately his decision — but that would have to be on the phone, and Marson hadn't got one yet. So he nodded Okay. He could start things off, anyway, he thought. Put out feelers.

'They'll have their heads down,' he said doubtfully.

Jeff shook his head. Foster was plugging things in, throwing switches. Dials glowed and meters flicked their fingers. A speaker on its back in the corner of his bench squawked once, then said: 'Ray — that you?'

Foster offered Marson a hand microphone, but Marson hesitated, unsure what to say. He'd had little contact with any of that crew.

Jeff rescued him. 'Let me.' Then he took the mike, shed a kind of formal skin, and was instantly affable, chatty.

'Rob! You old skinner.' How the hell he knew who it was, Marson couldn't guess. 'How's things?'

'Fine here,' said the speaker. 'Where are you Jeff?'

'At the river. We've got a spot of trouble.'

'We heard.' There was a note of authority in the voice, and Marson realised this was Robert Newby, Jeff's counterpart there, site foreman. 'I've been waiting here for a word from you, Jeff. You're going big on the radio, did you know?'

Jeff glanced at Foster, who shook his head. Probably he'd slept through the trip here. But Jeff was delighted. 'We are?'

'You want any help?'

'The team can handle it,' said Jeff, rather more confidently than Marson would have claimed. 'But we're short of a crane.'

'We guessed that.'

'And we thought of the Jones.'

'Yeah, of course. We reckoned you'd need a crane each side — '

'Let me have that,' Marson said quickly, reaching for the mike.

Jeff raised his eyebrows, but handed it over. Marson grabbed the mike.

'This is Colin Marson,' he said. 'Is your site manager available?'

A pause. Then the voice was more formal. 'He's at head office for a few days. But I can — '

'We need that Jones,' said Marson sharply. 'Need it urgently. As soon as I can get to a phone, I'll have a word with Sievewright, and he'll give you a release. I merely thought . . . as the Jones takes an hour or two to strip . . . you might start on *that* . . . ' It hadn't been firm, but it was a decision.

The loudspeaker jerked on the bench. 'Already doing that, Mr Marson. Nearly ready to go, as a matter of fact.'

'Go?'

Then another voice took over, a chipper voice, eager and brash. 'Hey there, Jeff. It's Marty.'

Marson held the mike, lost for a moment. Jeff leaned to it.

'Marty! Great to hear from you.'

'We're about ready to roll,' cried the voice. 'Coming along the footings, so be ready for us at the end. Gives you time to fix it with the boss. Eh . . . Jeff?'

'Who is this fool?' Marson asked, still holding the mike.

There was silence. The loudspeaker hummed.

'It's Marty Summers,' Jeff told him quietly. 'The Jones operator. Used to be with our team, when we had the Jones.'

'Tell him — '

'I'll try.' Jeff took the mike from him. 'You still there, Marty?'

'Who was that?' Suspicious and angry.

'My boss. Now listen. Calm down. We've got to get permission. Official. So sit tight and wait, Marty. All right?'

'We only do five miles an hour,' Marty protested in a high, injured voice.

'All the same . . . '

'You want it, don't you?'

Marson groaned. 'We want it,' he agreed, not realising Marty would hear.

'Then you're getting it.' And suddenly the radio was dead.

'Now look what you've done,' Jeff said.

Marson shrugged. He would be able to contact Sievewright in an hour or so, and in that time Marty would've moved only five miles. The situation was not irretrievable. He turned to the door. 'Where's this Charlie Maine of yours?'

Jeff was quiet and confident. 'I've already told him,' he said.

9

Laura lay awake on her bed, waiting for the click of the latch that would mean Den had gone to his own room. She could not relax, and as soon as she dozed she again heard him moving about in the living-room. It was still dark when she heard her father go out to the milking shed, but the two men did not speak to each other. Then she heard Den go out too, and a few minutes later the Ford pick-up starting. She hoped he'd be gone for the day, but she still couldn't relax properly, not with Johnny on the bridge. So she got up.

She made a pot of tea, but she couldn't eat a thing. When she went outside with a torch in her hand she discovered that Den had taken a couple of the big TV sets he'd got in the barn, and she hoped he'd gone searching for a buyer. That could well keep him out of the way for quite a while. She took the Mini and headed for the bridge.

The doctor was driving just in front of her along the road to the river. She watched him park, and followed him on foot to the cliff top, but not getting too close.

Her head was light and humming from lack

of sleep, and her mind was in a jumble, trying to get a firm line on her attitude to what was going on. That was the first time Chris went down to the cab. And there she'd been, all wrapped up in her own miseries, and he . . . She could see he was reluctant. They as good as shoved him out there, not giving him a chance. And it was terrifying, just to watch.

By that time she was caught in a small crowd of watchers, up around the hand winch, holding her breath, and when the whole thing just dropped she couldn't help screaming. Then one of the men pushed her and sent her flying, quite shaking her up, and when she looked again he was winding it in. She edged through, and saw them bring the doctor up, then she moved away. Way down the slope she saw somebody running away into the darkness.

Then she stayed. There wasn't anything to go home to. She stayed, getting soaked, and not caring. And watched. They had every available workman hard at it, though it was all a mystery to her. A strange little man with nice eyes started to drill holes in the rock, about fifteen yards back from the cliff edge, and explode little charges in them. The dust flew, and she could feel the tiny vibrations through the soles of her shoes. But she couldn't take her eyes from the bridge for long. Gently moving, sighing. She stood by one of the big chains, where it went over a pile of rocks, and she could hear it whispering away to itself. And Johnny was out there.

That was where she was when Grey came and stood by her. He was so tall. And that uniform. She'd always been a bit scared of policemen, and Den had never given up carping about them. This one was so sour that he terrified her. He looked cold, about dead on his feet, but give him his due he did try to be pleasant.

'You'll be Laura,' he said, nodding. 'I've heard about you.'

She wasn't feeling too good before that, and could only stare at him. Then away . . .

'I understand,' he went on chattily, 'that you know our friend out there.' But he'd managed to make it sound like a threat.

She couldn't think where that left her. 'He was coming to me,' she admitted.

'You're his wife?' As though he didn't believe a word of it.

She couldn't say she was. 'His name's Johnny Parfitt.'

When he didn't go on, she glanced up at him. It was the way he was so still that terrified her. She thought the light was moving across his face, then saw it was his jaw muscles moving.

'He was coming to me,' she said again.

'So you're not his wife,' he said, and she recalled that Chris had made a similar assumption. His voice had become tight. 'He got himself some strange transport to pay a visit — '

She tried to make it sound like more than a casual visit: 'I haven't seen him since . . . ' And just managed to stop herself.

He wouldn't let anything go. 'Since?' he insisted.

His steady eyes unnerved her, and she couldn't think of a decent lie. 'Since he went to prison,' she whispered.

'Ah.' He was nodding and nodding, and it seemed to her that he was excited, and tense. 'So it's *that* Johnny Parfitt.'

'What d'you mean 'that'?' She couldn't stop herself.

'Coming to you, you say? With a wagon-load of whisky?'

'It's his way. No, no — I didn't mean that. Not his way to steal it. He'd never do that. Never would, not for what was on it. But it's . . . it was his work, driving. That's all I meant.' And while she was saying it, she knew she was talking too much. She bit her lip, stopping herself.

'And whisky,' he muttered.

'I don't know what you mean.'

'It was whisky before,' he explained.

Then she could see that he knew all about it. He was staring into her brain with those bright, beady eyes of his and picking out every thought. He knew about Johnny and what had happened all those years ago, and he would come for Den and take him away, and then where would she be?

She laughed. How she got it out she didn't know. It must have sounded awful. 'Oh, you don't want to take any notice of that!' So light, so full of amusement. She felt ill. 'Johnny wouldn't be interested in what was on the wagon. He wouldn't want to keep it. Johnny isn't a thief.'

'Then what the hell d'you call him?' he asked, as though he was genuinely interested.

'He's . . . he's . . . ' She couldn't say it, couldn't think what Johnny was, except that she could remember the laughter and happy times and Johnny's strength and his strange, gentle pleasure with Harry. 'He's a good man,' she said, stupidly and weakly. 'But it's just the sort of thing he'd do, ridiculous Johnny, taking the first thing he could see, just to get home to me.'

But she knew she hadn't convinced him. He took off his cap and shook the drops from it, his eyes not leaving her.

'We'll have to ask him,' he said. 'When we get him out, we'll ask him where he was going with a wagonload of scotch. And perhaps we'll find it wasn't to you.'

'Yes, you do that,' she told him, trying to be defiant and confident. And for a while afterwards, watching the men working on the chairlift — and in the end throwing into the cab what looked like a small radio — she did think that what Grey had said was the idea behind it all: to ask Johnny where he'd been heading, with the question of rescuing him in the background. She was tired. Her thoughts were limping.

But the policeman had gone away, though not far enough for her liking.

They'd got a grubby old Land-rover on the top of the cliff, one with a canvas top, and it was covered all over with dents and rust marks. There was an old man working inside it, lying upside-down along the front seats. For a while she watched him, knowing she ought to go home. He grinned at her, his upper plate showing, and told her she looked like a drowned rat from where he was. And she supposed she did, at that.

'Going to ask him questions?' she asked, because she couldn't shake free of the idea.

He pulled himself upright and said: 'Not exactly ask. But we'll hear on this thing if he says anything. Though what good . . . ' He shook his head. 'But it was *his* idea, so that makes it law.'

He nodded towards the man she already knew to be in charge of it all — Colin Marson? Yes. To her, he didn't look big enough to be in charge of it. He knew how he wanted things, and he tried to make sure it was done as he instructed. But though they were all working away like mad, there wasn't any . . . well, certainty.

The old man climbed out of the Land-rover. He wasn't any taller than she was.

'Why don't you sit inside, missy, out of the rain?' he was good enough to suggest.

But she shook her head. She had to keep moving.

'And listen out for us?' he asked, cocking his head.

Oh, but she couldn't do that. Not listen for Johnny.

'No!' She knew it sounded a bit abrupt, so she gave him a weak version of a smile. 'I don't think I'd want to do that.'

But she was watching her, his old, pouched eyes very keen. 'We'll get him out. You'll see. You a friend of his?'

She nodded. 'Sort of.' He was only the father of her boy. 'Yes, I'm a friend.'

'Then you sit in here, love. I'll pass the

word around, and the lads'll leave you in peace.'

She was tempted. There were pains in her legs and back that she hadn't noticed before. But then Colin Marson marched across and said: 'You got it working yet, Foster?'

He wasn't glancing at her, not noticing her, she supposed, in his concentration.

'We're not gonna know that till he says something — are we, Mr Marson?' the old man asked, and Marson nodded, frowning.

'Well, you'd better get back to the radio van.' He looked at his watch. Then his eyes went over her. He looked her up and down. 'Who're you? You shouldn't be here. It's dangerous near this edge.'

'She's a friend of Johnny,' Foster said quickly.

'Oh.' He was considering her with more interest. 'It was you he was heading for, was it?'

She had to seize hold of that. 'Oh, yes.'

Then he suddenly smiled. It took away some of the tightness from his features, and his eyes came alive. He rubbed the back of his hand across his nose. 'Then make yourself useful, eh? How's about using the loudhailer, and talking to him?'

She saw it was hanging from his left hand. He'd been using it to call instructions across the river, so she already knew how loud it could be. 'Talking?' She didn't know whether he was serious.

'So that he'll know he's nearly made it, and you're here, waiting for him. Perhaps he can hear. If he says anything, we'll know that Foster here has done a good job.'

'But what could I say?' She felt hot with embarrassment.

Again he smiled. 'Tell him you love him, dear. Tell him you're waiting for him.'

'But . . . but everybody will hear.'

He pulled his ear lobe, then thrust the loudhailer at her. She couldn't help but take it. 'So what if they do? Maybe it'll help us all realise that there's a human being out there, and not just a pile of old iron.' He made a little gesture, almost as though he was apologising. 'And maybe,' he said quite quietly, 'it'll help Johnny. So what the hell does it matter what anybody thinks?'

She stood there like a fool. 'You press that button,' he explained. She did that, and lifted it to her lips, and whispered: 'Johnny! Can you hear me? It's Laura.'

It went in as a whisper and came bouncing out as a great shout. The men stopped working and lifted their heads, one or two smiling. She felt defiant, and tried again.

'Johnny, it's Laura. Can you speak to me? Please!'

Then all she could hear was the roar of the river, the occasional groan of the metal, because the hammering and shouting and the banging of those little explosions stopped. They were all waiting, and behind her, in the Land-rover, she could hear the hiss of the radio, and then, suddenly, a break in that sound, a sob and a whimper that was as piercing as a full-throated cry. She couldn't hold back a choked cry for herself, and dropped the loudhailer. Marson grabbed for it, and as he straightened up she clung to his shoulder. They stood together like that.

The loudspeaker sound couldn't have reached many of the men, but Marson put the loudhailer to his lips and called out: 'We're in touch. He's okay. Let's get on with it.'

He didn't let her try again at that time. Her legs felt like putty, but she could no more have sat in that cab. She had to walk away. A few of the men nodded and smiled at her, but she was unable to smile back. Not even at the two or three men who were walking around with television cameras on their shoulders. Somebody thrust a microphone in her face, but she flinched away, and he shrugged.

It must have been about midday. She knew

119

she ought to get back and cook her dad's dinner, but he always said he could manage. She was hypnotised by the bridge, and couldn't move far from it. While she stood watching, the old man called Foster came limping up the slope, shouting: 'He's on the radio, Mr Marson.'

'Radio?' Marson seemed a little slow on the uptake.

'Mr Sievewright. He's at the main site.'

'Oh Christ!' And Marson hurried away, looking anxious.

She didn't know what it meant, but couldn't take her eyes from him. He was half running down towards the collection of caravans and vehicles.

Then a man at her elbow spoke. 'I'm wondering if it shouldn't be stopped.'

'Stopped!' she cried out. 'But Johnny's out there.'

Then she recognised him. He was Frank Allison, who'd done all the hard work trying to stop the motorway from coming through. He'd lost a lot of weight since she'd seen him last, and he had that look in his eyes they all get — a fanatic. Worry, worry, worry. They all go crazy in the end, she thought. He was staring at her solemnly, nodding.

'Ah. You'll be his lady-friend.'

She wasn't going to be taken in by his

friendly tone. 'He was coming home to me.'

'A bit foolish, perhaps, to choose this bridge.' He smiled wearily. 'Though I understand he was trying to evade the police.'

'That makes it different, does it?' she asked him bitterly. 'That makes him a criminal, so's nobody's got to worry about him?'

'Not a criminal, perhaps. Shall we say anti-social?'

Everything he'd said had been in a gentle voice, and as she'd been furious with him it made him sound sad for her. She made an effort to be very calm.

'You're a solicitor,' she said. 'It's your job, playing around with words,' she said. 'But you're not going to get me arguing with you, because you'll only prove I'm selfish, just for praying they'll rescue Johnny.'

He smiled, but it did no more than distort his features. 'I'd never say that, my dear. Of course you're selfish. Anyone in your position would be just aching.' Then he put his fingers to his lips. 'They haven't told you about the cliffs?'

'Nobody's told me anything,' she complained. 'What about them?'

'I have it on good authority . . . ' All pompous. ' . . . if you can call Colin Marson a good authority — on his word, then — that the weight of all that metal and whisky out

there is pulling down the cliffs. Not yet — '
He had noticed how startled she was ' — but
gradually. And of course, if it did, the valley
above here would be completely flooded.'

She supposed it was his formal court voice.
No feeling in it. She started at him, then told
him: 'Our farm's two or three miles back.'

He was very gentle. 'I know, my dear. I
remember — from the motorway inquiry.'

So what did he want her to stay? 'All right
then,' she burst out. 'So I'm selfish. I don't
care if the cliffs come down.' So there, she
thought.

'But it'd take Johnny with it,' he pointed
out.

He'd done it after all, got her tied-up with
his smooth words. She had said what she
didn't mean, but somehow she'd felt what he
was getting at — that Johnny had been
anti-social in trying to cross the bridge, and
now was being even more anti-social by being
stubborn and staying alive. She too, she
supposed, by praying for him.

'What d'you want me to say?' she asked,
and suddenly she was desperately tired.
'What will make you happy?'

'Happy is hardly the word.'

'Relieved, then. What d'you want — that
they'll stop doing what they're doing, and
. . . what then?'

And then she realised he hadn't been asking her anything, he'd just been talking to himself, playing with the two sides of the argument. And he was losing both ways. There was pain in the line of his mouth.

'I want something,' he said quietly, 'completely outside all moral inclinations.' His voice seemed so distorted that she barely understood him. He was turning away. 'Something . . . ' His voice floated away. ' . . . unthinkable.'

She watched him go. He was walking aimlessly. Then he seemed to lift his head, and he made for the cluster of caravans.

Passing him, on his way up to the cliff, was Chris Keene.

10

Jeff Fisher told Chris that Marson had been called to the radio. Jeff was all for getting on with it — meaning Chris's part in the big effort. He had Cropper with him, and from what Chris was able to make out they were thinking up a few fancy ideas. Chris nudged Cropper's elbow.

'I didn't get a chance to thank you properly,' he said, and Cropper simply looked embarrassed and mumbled: 'Nothin' to it.'

Jeff cut in. 'This is what we thought. It was Cropper's idea, really. He reckons he could cut the whole driver's door out in a couple of minutes. Then you could really get at him.'

They were looking at him like a couple of eager kids, and he sensed how much his approval meant to them. 'And what does Colin say about it?' he asked.

Jeff shrugged. 'Oh, he says we'd never get Johnny out, with all that metalwork trapping his foot, and with the door missing . . . but they do it in motorway crashes, cut 'em out. Take off a limb, if they have to.' He was talking glibly, not allowing himself to visualise what he was saying. 'We could ask for the team.' He was silent.

Chris could see that there must have been strong words between Jeff and Marson. He nodded. 'He's correct there, Jeff. It'd mean something drastic. And with the door missing, we'd be losing too much heat. We've got to keep him warm, and if the wind veered enough it'd be blowing rain on him. No. Better leave the door alone for now. And can you really see an operating team out there? We need some other way we can get at him. He'll be dehydrated, so I'll have to get a drip working, and I ought to get a close look at that foot of his.' He turned to Cropper. 'How about a smaller hole, right opposite the foot pedals? A foot square, say. Could you do that?'

Cropper nodded. 'Sure could.'

'Is there room for two of us on that thing?' he asked, as though his heart wasn't thumping.

They had improved the chairlift, but it still looked frail. There was now a thin rail round the back and sides, which might have been enough to stop his bag slipping off. It wouldn't hold him, though, if the thing tilted.

'You an' me?' said Cropper. 'Just about.'

Cropper's words seemed to comfort Chris. He was trying as hard as he could to share the others' confidence. The solid presence of the man who had just saved his life was probably as close as he could get to reassurance out on that death trap. Then, as if suddenly noticing that something was missing, he began to look about him anxiously. 'Isn't Colin going to be here?'

Jeff sounded serious. 'I saw him go into the radio shack. That was ten minutes ago. I reckon he's tied up.'

Chris moistened his lips. There was a metallic taste in his mouth, as though he'd been sucking a penny, and a high hard pain between his eyes. 'You want us to go without him?'

'We'll be fine.' Jeff's reach for a casual tone rang a little hollow.

The pallor deepened in Chris's cheeks. 'But — '

'Tell you what,' Jeff interrupted, keen to get on with it before Marson emerged, 'we'll rig you up a safety line.'

'A what?' said Cropper.

'A safety line. We could take it over the pulley and pay it out.'

'Not for me.' Cropper was more curt than ever. 'It'd get in the way.'

'Of course not for you,' Jeff replied impatiently. 'Just for the doctor.'

Chris nodded. The fear with which he had held on to those rapidly slackening ropes, the sick lurch in the centre of his body as the fragile plank had plummeted, were fresh in his mind. A safety line would keep him alive, whatever happened. 'Okay. A safety line.'

Cropper had the line rigged within minutes. Jeff slipped the loop under Chris's arms and gave it a sharp tug, as if making a promise. There was still no sign of Colin.

'So, let's go Cropper. You and the doctor. You got your gas bottles?'

Cropper made a gesture of lifting the two small gas bottles — not more than a foot long, clanking together, one black, one red. The plank was just about wide enough, so Cropper wedged the bottles together and held his outfit on his knees, Chris held his bag on his. He took a deep breath, feeling the blood run from his cheeks. Then they were away.

The chair felt much more steady. Chris decided it was the extra weight, though every now and again he would reach for the certainty of his lifeline. The rain continued, and the wind remained slight. As he watched the cab approach, the terror he had had for himself was gradually replaced by the fear he felt for Johnny.

'Sit tight,' he said, as they came opposite the cab. 'Signal them up a bit. I've got to check how he is, before we do anything.'

The chair rose a foot. That seemed fine. No need for perching on his toes, and he knew where he'd left Johnny's wrist. As he reached down and found it, he realised with a sinking heart that it proved Johnny had not moved.

Johnny's pulse was weak but even, his skin clammy. Before they went any further, Chris was determined to get some antibiotic into him, and tried desperately to get far enough inside to reach his chest with the stethoscope.

'You come outa there,' said Cropper suddenly. 'It don't sound good.'

Chris remained very still for a few moments. Cropper was right. There had been a change in the bridge's note of protest, a deeper groan from the metal. And he'd been a foot short of Johnny's chest.

'Then be quiet,' he said.

But listening didn't help. He couldn't hear Johnny's breathing for the roar of the river, and now, reaching for silence, it seemed to him that the bridge's complaints were louder than ever.

He gave it up, lowered himself to the seat, and prepared a couple of syringes.

'What you doin'?' Cropper asked. He seemed uneasy.

'Two injections first. Antibiotic and pain-killer. It's a risk, giving him painkiller, because I haven't been able to check his

128

respiration. But he's got to have it. Then I'll get a drip going. That's going to be the most difficult.'

'And this part ain't?'

Chris looked at him. Cropper was watching Chris's hands, which were shaking. 'It's all right,' Chris said, but Cropper shook his head, and for a moment looked back to the solid comfort of the cliffs.

'The wagon would come down on top of us,' he said dully. It was no more than a comment, something for Chris to bear in mind.

He got to his feet, giving Cropper one of the syringes. 'Hand it up when I say.'

He had done it before. Practice makes perfect. One needle in, toss the syringe away, reach down for Cropper's — water pouring from Cropper's face, his eyes slits — then the other in. There was no time for hygiene, and anyway, from the smell, he knew there could be something worse to come.

The drip was terrible to get in. It isn't easy to get a drip going, even with modern equipment, quietly beside a hospital bed. You have to find a vein, slip the tube in accurately, withdraw the metal liner and leave the plastic tube in place, and rig up the drip so that there are no bubbles in it, nothing to interrupt the flow, with the whole thing adjusted to one drip a second. Chris was using a saline-dextrose base, hoping it would last four hours without any tissuing.

There was no alternative but to get both shoulders inside and use both hands, and it had to be taped in position when he had it working. Time slid away. Cropper was protesting weakly all the while, and indistinct mumble of the loudhailer was going mad. But Jeff didn't have to do it, and somebody had to, and in the end he was back on his feet on the chairlift, with only the plastic bottle to support.

He hooked the bottle to the rim around the top edge of the cab, pleased, nearly satisfied, and aware that he had one thing he could replace over and over. Or so he thought at the time.

As he sat down, Cropper whipped the rain from his face with one hand. 'You going to do that every time?'

'That or something like it.'

'Can you do it on your own?'

'Better with a good weight like you, Cropper, holding it steady.' Chris tried to grin, but his face ached.

'Why d'you have to say things like that?' Cropper grumbled.

'Now,' Chris said, 'let's get on. Time for your bit. About there, I'd say.'

With his head inside, he'd been able to associate the position of Johnny's feet with the bodywork. He indicated a square in the metal immediately in front of the door. Rainwater was pouring over it.

Cropper's head was close to his. 'How far is his foot?' he asked, his eyes moving. 'Behind this lot, I mean.'

'Three inches. Six, perhaps.'

'But I can't . . . ' Cropper started again. 'Don't you know how far this flame goes?'

'I'll get up there with my torch and I'll guide the flame inside. Tell you up and down and so on. Okay?'

Cropper looked doubtful. 'If you say so.'

'I've got to get a good look at that foot.'

Cropper nodded. Chris got to his feet. When he glanced down, Cropper was on his knees, the flame going. He reached inside with the hand torch, his head in. The flame struck through, and he saw exactly what Cropper had meant, as it had shot out only inches from the leg, spottles of molten metal flying with it.

'A bit to your right,' he called quickly.

And so on. It was painfully slow. They had to keep breaking off, and Cropper's face was red with strain and heat. They had nearly finished when Chris heard a snap of metal, as though something had broken. It seemed to come from close to his head. He levered his head out of the cab, and looked.

There was a small, round hole six inches from the drip bottle. There was a plucked hole in the shoulder of his anorak, the wadding pulled out. He stared at it, not understanding. Then it happened again, a foot farther away, and suddenly and appallingly he knew. Somebody was shooting at them.

The blood hit the top of his head with a smack, and his eyes went out of focus. He wanted to scream, but Cropper was on the last cut. He couldn't stop him now, didn't dare to let anyone know. There'd be panic . . .

He got down quickly to his knees. The square plate was coming out. Anxious to be away from there, he reached out to bend it free, but Cropper slapped his hand away. Chris saw he was wearing thick, rubberised gloves. Cropper lifted the piece out and tossed it away. He seemed to be taking an eternity, and the flesh crawled up Chris's back.

He lowered his head, the flame-cutter hissing beside his ear, and tried to forget the shots and the delicate balance of the bridge, and his own fear. The foot was crushed, bone showing through the flesh. A shaft of cast iron seemed to be piercing the side of Johnny's boot. The visible flesh was dark, the smell putrescent. There was nothing he could do. In all that mess, nothing.

'We'll have to get back,' he croaked.

'Let me see.'

'No. It's bad. We haven't got much time. Signal us in.'

They were brought in slowly. Chris was shaking, the tension flowing from him. Every yard was drawn-out agony. He staggered onto the cliff surface, and it was Marson who was there with the loudhailer, looking grim.

'You've got to hurry, Colin,' Chris said, still not certain whom he should tell about the shots. 'He's bad, really bad.'

'If you say so.' Marson sounded dull.

'Get your stuff rigged,' Chris told him. 'Get your crane here.'

Marson turned away, giving a shout to the air. 'I want you, Jeff.'

Grey was at Chris's elbow, looking grave, though somehow excited, and his eyes were on the plucked tear in the anorak.

'You've got to keep him alive.' It was a flat instruction.

'I'm trying.'

Then Chris looked at Grey as if for the first time. He was strange. No doubt he'd been there, at the cliff, for twelve solid hours. The exhaustion was showing, breaking him down.

But his last remark had not been pure routine or duty. There had been a personal ring to it, as though the outcome had become intensely important to him.

'Alive,' Chris agreed. 'For you?'

Grey took his arm and led him aside. 'D'you know what I thought I heard? Shots. Ridiculous, I know. Perhaps I'm feeling the strain too.' His finger reached out, and he gently flicked the protruding padding on Chris's shoulder. 'Perhaps not, though.'

Chris took a breath, looking round for somewhere to sit. 'I've been shot at,' he said, his voice shaking.

'Does anyone else know?' Grey asked, dipping his head and peering at him under the peak.

'I'm reporting it to you. For God's sake, man, shot at!'

'Not at *you*, doctor. Nothing personal, I'm sure. He was probably aiming at the drip bottle.' Grey was calm — unbelievably calm. It was the calmness of contained triumph.

'He?' Chris demanded. 'You *know* him?'

'Calm down. Don't make a scene.' Grey put a hand to his elbow. 'Here, you'd better sit down. Let's get in the Land-rover.'

Chris did as Grey suggested, but shook his hand off. 'What the hell's going on?'

Grey was in the driver's seat, the skirts of

his mac pulled up. He took off his cap and looked down at it. His voice was very quiet. 'I don't know who he is. I've been waiting for four years to find out. Patience, that's what makes a good policeman. And now — *this* is going to bring him to me, make him show himself. The moment I found out what was on that truck, I was ready for him. And when I heard the name of Johnny Parfitt, I knew I was close.'

Reaching for a cigarette, Chris glanced at him uneasily. 'That bullet was close,' he said quietly.

'And so was the business with the winch slipping.'

'You mean it was the same . . . ?'

Grey was nodding.

'You said nothing bloody personal!' Chris shouted.

'Keep your voice down. I'll explain. That Johnny Parfitt was involved in a hijack, just over four years ago. He was driving a wagon-load of whisky. Six tons of it. Whisky, you see. That hijack. Parfitt was driving the wagon, and he chose to take a lonely road. He was in with them, of course, and I suppose the idea was to tap him on the head to make it look genuine. But it wasn't the sort of road for a wagon. One of our patrol cars noticed it and followed, just curious you understand.

But they saw that tap on the head, and they went in. The wagon got away, with a man standing on the back of the load. The patrol car stopped to pick up Parfitt, then they went in pursuit.'

It sounded to Chris like an official report.

'The co-driver in the patrol car said later that they could've been doing sixty. There was no chance of getting past on that narrow road, so they were hustling the wagon, trying to force them into error. And all the time that jeering devil on the back . . .

'He picked up a crate of scotch and hurled it at the car's windscreen. You can imagine what that did, at sixty. Parfitt and the co-driver got a period in hospital. The driver was killed. Parfitt would never reveal the identity of the man on the wagon, and yet he must have known him. No amount of . . . '

'Pressure?' Chris suggested, as Grey tried to find the word.

'Interrogation,' Grey corrected severely. 'Nothing we could do would persuade him. He went on trial for complicity to manslaughter, and got seven years. So now he's out, with remission, and he's in that wagon out there. When I knew who he was, I had the vague idea that he'd been taking this wagon to the same man.'

'Would he do that?' asked Chris. 'He'd

hardly consider him a friend.'

'You're quite right. Just as I reasoned it. But then, I thought, when we get him out, then he'll be ready to give us a name.'

'I don't see that.' Chris was short with him. Grey's objective didn't appeal. 'Why should he, when he wouldn't before?'

'Having served his sentence, maybe ... no, I don't think he will either. But, clearly, that's what my man thinks, and that's all that matters. Look at it, and see what's happened. The media, the TV people, the radio — for once in their narrow, sordid lives they've done some good. Somewhere, listening to the news, our character from the whisky wagon has heard that Johnny Parfitt is here, trapped, and in the circumstances likely to reveal his name. If we get him out alive. So, he's come to me. I don't have to search him out, he's coming to me. At first — the winch — I had a thought, a hope that it could be him. But now — the shots — damn it, it must be him. He daren't allow me to rescue Parfitt alive.'

Chris noted sourly that it was Grey who was doing the rescuing.

'You mean,' suggested Chris, 'dare not allow *me* to keep him alive?'

'You mustn't think that. Purely impersonal, I assure you.'

'It was a personal bullet.'

'Oh please, not that attitude.'

'Attitude? You're going to sit here like a bleeding spider, waiting, waiting, while he picks at me — picks at anybody — with his rifle, or whatever he's got.'

'Which is exactly why I'm asking you to be very discreet. Not a word. I don't want him to know I know.'

'I can't believe I'm hearing this.'

'And anyway, can you imagine they'd all go on working, with the danger?'

'So there is a danger? You concede that much?'

'They'd see it as such. But you're more sensible than that. Now I'm on the alert. The whole of my resources will be concentrated on this. We can trap him like that!' His palm slapped down on his knee.

'Is that what makes a policeman?' Chris asked in disgust.

Grey's eyes darted from side to side. 'He's here, somewhere. The danger, if that's how you prefer to see it, is still there. Would I do better going after him, when I haven't got a clue where to look, and leaving this area unprotected? Ask yourself that.'

'You expect me to go down there, knowing some madman's got a rifle?'

'But I'll get him first. Believe me.' Grey

spoke with a stubborn persistence that was almost manic.

'And all this effort, what's it going to get you? Promotion?'

'Satisfaction. Retribution.' His voice was cold and thin. 'He murdered my son. My son drove that police car. My son, four years dead.'

11

It wasn't going well, and Marson knew it. They were up to schedule, perhaps a little ahead. But the most important thing was the Jones. He grew more and more nervous the longer he went without contacting Sievewright. He used the ten-hundredweight van to drive to the nearest phone box, but they told him that Sievewright had left his office in a hurry. He was therefore almost relieved when Foster told him that Sievewright was on the radio. But Marson realised it meant Sievewright was at the main site.

Ray Foster was looking nervous when he handed over the mike. Before Marson pressed the transmit button he nodded for Foster to leave. He was left alone with Foster's mongrel, who eyed him with suspicion.

'Marson,' he said.

'About time, too. What the hell's this with the Jones?'

Thomas Winstanley Sievewright, that was, self-made man, founder and overlord of Sevco Corporation, and in a bad mood.

'You'll realise why we need a bigger crane,'

Marson said. 'You'll have heard about it — '

'Heard enough, Marson. Why the devil you let yourself get involved, Christ knows. It's not *ours*, man. There's an official way of going about this sort of thing. You're on a loser, you've got yourself conned into it. Lack of field experience. You'll learn, though. In the meantime, you've got to come along and speak to that fool on the Jones. He just ploughs ahead. Insane, I think.'

He was ignoring the whole situation into non-existence. There was only one way to squash that: plough ahead.

'You'll have seen, Chief, on the telly, seen what it's like,' Marson said. 'We don't stand a chance without the Jones crawler.'

His bark of contempt almost split the speaker. 'Not a chance. We don't want any fiascos, Marson. Nothing like that, linked with the company. So speak to your man on the Jones. We need it here, on the main site, and you bloody well know it.'

'But I can't just — '

'You heard. Do it, for Christ's sake, and stop arguing.'

The speaker clicked when he switched off, and Marson stood there, mike in hand. He knew what it was all about. Head office stank with it — one of the reasons he'd been glad to get away from there. Sievewright didn't want the company involved. He *knew* they were going to fail, and that was all right as long as it was Marson's operation. Send in equipment from the main site, and it would become a company affair, and Sievewright was afraid of that. He'd change his tune when they succeeded. If they succeeded. Then it would be Sievewright beaming on the screen, and claiming it all for himself.

The radio came on again suddenly. 'Jeff?'

'It's not Jeff,' Marson said wearily. 'It's Marson.'

'Sorry about all that, but he's been raving, here. We can't do a tap, and Marty Summers just keeps the Jones moving. Nobody can stop him.'

Marson could imagine that. The Jones probably weighed fifty tons. Get that moving, and you'd need an anti-tank gun to stop it. 'I'll drive over and speak to him,' he said wearily.

He put the mike down on the bench. The mongrel put his ears back as he went out.

He watched them bringing in Chris and Cropper. They had taken a square foot of metal from the side of the cab. Whatever they had achieved, however it might help, it was nothing compared to what Marson would have to do to ensure the availability of the Jones. He had to leave now to head off the

Jones, to keep Sievewright reasonable. He told Jeff what he wanted doing while he was away. There seemed little point in making Sievewright's objections known — in making the team doubt the worth of his every order — until he had tried everything, exhausted all his options.

It had been just under two hours since he had spoken to Marty Summers, so the Jones would have travelled nearly ten miles. With the large-scale map of the proposed motorway route, he was able to calculate within a hundred yards where the Jones would be at that moment. Ahead of the main team, Marson's advance team had been laying the rough foundations. He searched out the nearest ordinary road that the footings intersected. Then he took the van and headed there.

He was leaving all the problems to Jeff. He knew that he should have been doing all he could to find some kind of contingency plan that wouldn't involve the Jones, but he refused to face it. He chose the path of least resistance, talked himself into a adopting a mental block: however difficult it would be to procure the Jones, it was easier than even contemplating the consequences of having to work without it. He was driving blindly, and probably too fast. The minor road came to a sudden end, and he spotted the Jones at once.

Its engine note, flat out, split the countryside as uncompromisingly as the motorway itself. The Jones was coming on, its track rolling and crunching, its boom laced high over the cab in its folded position, tall plumes of black smoke jetting from the exhaust. Marson stood and waited. It took just over a minute to cover the intervening 150 yards, and the roar deafened him.

He sprang on to the back and allowed the top of the track to roll him forward to the cab. There was room for only one inside. The exhaust was a foot from his head, and seemed to be splitting his skull. He opened the door and ducked his head in.

He didn't know Marty Summers. To his surprise he saw that Summers would have been around sixty, when his impression had been of a younger man. But apart from age, he'd found out a few things about Marty. He had worked on the advance team with Big Jim for years, and had taken over the Jones crawler when it first came into service. But time progresses and things change. When he'd been offered the faster and more versatile Kato hydraulic crane, Big Jim hadn't hesitated. He took it, and offered its seat to Marty. But to Marty the Jones was *his*. He'd lived in it and for it. So he had chosen to stay with the Jones, even though it meant leaving Big Jim, and now Marson had the impression that Marty thought he was heading back to his old boss.

'I'm Colin Marson,' he bellowed. 'Site boss of the advance team.'

Marty nodded. 'Yeah. Yeah.' Marson had to read his lips, and he thrust his head in closer. Then he could read Marty's eyes.

To Marty, Big Jim would have been a god. He'd worshipped him only second to his beloved Jones. So, the decision to abandon the crane or Big Jim must have been traumatic. He had chosen the Jones, so had not been on site when Big Jim was killed. They say that nobody really dies until the last person who remembers him with affection also dies. That was how it must have been with Marty. Big Jim was alive in his mind, and the memory of those grand old days when Big Jim, the team, and the Jones were all together, had grown in his mind to a nostalgic perfection which he longed to return to, yearned for.

And now, the opportunity had been presented. Marty and his Jones crawler were needed by his old team of mates. What a wonderful thing it is to be needed! All that would be missing from the package was Big Jim himself, and maybe Marty wasn't aware of that in his excited euphoria. Imagine the shock when what he got was Marson.

That was what Marson saw in those eyes — shock. Big, hazel eyes Marty had, under a mass of untidy, nearly white hair, and a long, thin face. Almost mournful, that was the first impression. But there was fire in the back of those eyes, and suddenly a deadly fear. This stranger he saw was going to tell him he was not needed, to turn him round and send him back. His mouth tightened as he braced himself.

'Sievewright's playing hell,' Marson shouted. 'Nobody *told* you to take this thing away.'

Marty's hands danced on the two levers as he expressed himself. His mouth went square as he shouted: 'There's a bloke on . . . that . . . bridge. You're gonna . . . need us.'

The engine drummed Marson's head into stupidity. 'Stop the engine!' He was already losing his voice. 'I can't talk — '

'Ya want us, don't y'?' There was nothing lacking in Marty's voice. At the full stretch of his lungs, it still contained as much entreaty as it would if he'd sobbed it.

'You can't just drive.' Marson tried to reason with him.

'You get outa my cab!' Marty told him

forcefully. 'See if I can't.'

'It's illegal. He'll get the police to stop you. You'll be chucked out on your ear. Do you understand me, Marty? I've been told to turn you back. I've got to do that.'

Marty turned to look at Marson again. He'd got every word of that. His contempt expressed his opinion of each one.

'Get on with it then,' Marty shouted, managing to sneer at the top of his voice.

They were going to get the Jones at Prescott's Bridge, whatever anybody said or did, however many police cars he had to plough into the ground, even if he had to roll right over Sievewright himself.

Marson put his head close to Marty's, his mouth to his ear. 'I've said it all. Keep going, friend.'

He jumped down, and walked back the 200 yards they had traversed. The engine behind him rasped in defiance, and perhaps exultation.

At the end of that 200 yards, Sievewright was waiting for him.

'He's not turning, Marson.'

'No.'

'Was that your instruction?'

Marson offered no reply.

He laughed in Marson's face. 'Lord, but you're a fool. I gave you a direct order, and you've ignored it. You'll regret that, you know. You'll never work again in this country, if I — '

'You know damn well why I've got to have the Jones.'

Sievewright lifted his head. 'I'll simply turn it back.'

Marson grinned at him, wondering how far Sievewright could be pressed. 'But would you dare? With the publicity we're getting . . . ' He allowed it to tail off, leaving it to Sievewright's imagination.

Sievewright had been smooth and almost polite up to that moment. Now it all disappeared. Marson thought for a moment that he'd strike him.

'Don't you threaten *me*, Marson.'

'Your threat came first.'

'You're not big enough,' Sievewright said viciously. 'Not for this job, not for playing games with me. I'll take you off it — put somebody else — '

'Who else? Who?'

'I'll dismiss you. Damn it, you *are* dismissed.'

'Go to hell!' Marson shouted at him, then he slammed his way into the van.

Jeff looked at him strangely when he got back. Marson could remember nothing of the return journey. His mind was a chaos of anger, trepidation — and excitement, he supposed.

Jeff merely said: 'We're mixing the first run of concrete.'

The big mixer was growling away, and they were laying the footings for the mounting bolts.

'The Jones is on its way,' Marson said, surprised how calm his voice sounded.

There had never, as far as Jeff was aware, been any doubt over the Jones's course. He eyed his boss curiously, wondering where he had just been, guessing at the information he was withholding. A more experienced site boss would have known the importance of sharing his knowledge with his team. Jeff had come to know the way Marson worked, the ego that governed the man. It was as if Marson thought that by keeping the most important facts to himself he would ensure his involvement in every aspect of the operation; that he alone would hold the key to their every success. But Jeff knew that there was no time to overcome the obstacles — both physical and psychological — that such an attitude presented. If Marson insisted on his need-to-know approach, the glory he sought would fall to pieces in his hands. He alone would hold the key to their failure.

Now was not the time. Jeff continued to update him. 'The cliff's moving,' he said.

'I know.'

'I mean, you can measure it.'

'I know.'

'I mean, we ought to measure it. To see how much time we've got left.' Jeff was choosing his words as carefully as he could.

'You want me to start a graph? Now?'

'It would keep the locals quiet. That Allison's been looking for you.' Marson paused for a moment, amusing himself by struggling — and failing — to think of anyone he wanted to see less than Allison. His small smile was interrupted by the sound of a man clearing his throat behind them. They turned around. It was Allison.

There's always one around, Marson thought sourly, the self-appointed representative of all those people who didn't want representing. He approached, a light of battle in his eyes. Or misery, rather. Allison was miserable at the thought of battle.

'I'm not sure I like this,' he said.

'I'm not too pleased myself,' Marson assured him.

'The cliff's moving. You can almost feel it.'

Marson tried to be patient. 'It'll slide, Mr Allison. Gently. In a steady acceleration. We'll have plenty of time to make decisions.'

'By that, you mean that you will.'

'If you like, yes, me.' This was a new line of approach, and Marson sensed danger.

'That's what worries me,' Allison said mournfully, so lost in his self-torture that he didn't realise how insulting it sounded. 'It shouldn't be left to one man.'

'What shouldn't?' Marson was forcing him into stating it.

'Whether to go on with this, and possibly bring down the cliffs, or cut it free now — or at any rate before it gets too bad.'

'What d'you suggest then?' He managed that in a nicely controlled voice.

'A committee.'

Marson looked past him. The bridge moved uneasily. Every now and then the woman cried out something with a loud-hailer, and he could see a man on the far cliff risking his life erecting a tripod. 'It's the same argument,' he said flatly, 'as a firing squad. No single person is supposed to know who has done the killing. But that's a fallacy, because they all did.'

Allison looked shrunken, his face rigid with strain. 'It's not quite — '

'I'll get you a graph going,' Marson said tightly. 'Then you'll be able to time it — you and your committee. We'll put a notice on the parish board: the time we're going to kill

151

Johnny Parfitt. It'll be just like a hanging — they can all come and watch.'

Allison looked at him sadly — pitying him, Marson thought — shaking his head. They stood there a couple of minutes in silence, then Allison turned and went away.

'Johnny,' she was saying, 'You're going to be all right. We're going to get you out of there.'

At Marson's feet the crack had slipped a quarter of an inch since he'd looked last. He shouted for somebody to start taking hourly readings.

12

She was there all day. The men were wonderful to her. There would've been about thirty in the team, and most of them had been up since two in the morning, but they always managed a friendly word when they came near. And a laugh. Every now and then they'd take her down to their mobile canteen for a sandwich and a drink, and they even offered her the use of a caravan for a rest, but she didn't dare close her eyes. They were gentlemen. Rough and big and noisy, but they were gentle and they were real men.

The doctor came back in the afternoon. She watched him go down to Johnny again, alone, though Cropper wanted to go with him. She could see that he was afraid, and trying not to give way to that sort of thing. You don't have to give way, she said to herself. It was because of fear that she'd always given way to Den, and she didn't find that thought pleasant, because she wasn't sure that what she was doing at the bridge wasn't just damned selfish after all. She was anxious to help save Johnny, but wasn't it because he could tell her where they'd taken

Harry? And if she knew where, she'd be able to . . .

But she wasn't sure what she could do about Den, because that sort of fear grows right into your veins.

Chris came back, shattered again, and terribly white. She ran to him, and he was shaking his head, meaning that for a moment he wasn't able to speak.

'It's all right,' he said. 'There's been no change.'

'It frightens you,' she said.

He managed to smile, but she could see it was an effort. 'It's not just the bridge,' he told her.

Her heart was suddenly beating terribly. 'Then what?'

He took her arm and walked with her, away from the bridge and the men. 'All the time I'm down there,' he said, 'every second, I'm expecting something.'

She stumbled, and he took her weight with his fingers. 'I don't understand.' She made sure he didn't see her face.

'There's a feeling going around,' he told her, his voice very deep. 'Around the district. You must have heard it. A feeling that the lower farms are in danger from the cliffs. Somebody, somewhere, wants Johnny dead, so that they could drop the bridge into the

154

river and the cliffs would be safe.'

He was so close to the truth. She couldn't help making a suppressed cry. He stopped. 'So you know about it?' He took her arm, holding her still.

She nodded, waiting, and fearing how much he might have found out — or guessed.

He went on: 'And that same person is prepared to kill me, if I try too hard for Johnny.'

She told herself this was no more than dramatics. He was really quite ugly, she saw, in an attractive way. But he was no good at telling lies, and that was what he was doing. Or at least, not telling all the truth.

'The superintendent's got other ideas,' he said doubtfully. 'But I don't think he's quite sane.'

It was almost as though nothing was real, there on the heath, with Chris coming out with it so calmly. 'What does he think?' she asked, trying to be as calm as Chris.

He shrugged. 'It's an obsession. Forget it.'

He began to walk ahead again. They were making a circle of the encampment. He seemed to have said all he was going to.

'Is that all you wanted to say?' she asked, with a jerk at his arm, pretending to a lightness she didn't feel.

'I was hoping to persuade you to go home,'

he said gravely. 'You're exhausted, and under great strain.'

'I can't leave him now.'

'He's not responding.'

'I thought he was. There've been odd times . . . ' She stopped, her throat thick.

'I can't take on any more patients, Laura,' he said.

'I'm not on your books.'

'You're on my mind. I need to leave it clear for Johnny.'

They walked a few more yards, then she said: 'You don't have to worry about me. I'll stay around a bit longer.'

'He means that much to you?'

She considered how to answer that. 'I loved Johnny, very dearly. I try to remember it, but somehow I can't feel the same.'

'Then why, Laura, are you making yourself ill for him?'

He was always being dramatic. 'Not specially for Johnny,' she told him. 'More for my son.'

That stopped him. His fingers were painful on her arm. 'Yes,' he said. 'You mentioned a child.'

She smiled at the relaxation in his voice. 'He'll be five now, Harry. Johnny's boy. He was born a year before it . . . his arrest happened. It . . . ' How could she put it without mentioning Den?

'It wasn't a good thing, just at that time, to have Harry with me at the farm, so I asked Johnny's parents to take him for a while. They were pleased. Nice people, though I don't think they cared much for me.'

She knew it didn't sound very sensible, the way she was telling it. She wasn't putting it over quite as it seemed to her. He seemed to notice and grimaced to help her. 'I can see what's coming,' he said.

'Oh, you mustn't think badly of them,' she said quickly, trying to justify what the Parfitts had done. 'Their only trouble is that they're not exactly honest. I suppose it runs in the family. Anyway, the police were looking for them, and they just upped and offed — with Harry. That was two years ago, and I still haven't found out.'

'But that's quite fantastic,' he burst out. 'You're not suggesting they're deliberately . . . no, of course not. But surely, the police . . . '

'I told you, they were already looking for them.'

'This is terrible. Haven't they written to you?'

'They're not too good at writing. The odd postcard, once from Aberdovey, I remember. I wondered at that time if they were in a touring caravan. I wouldn't say they'll *never* bring him back to me . . . '

'I should hope not.'

'But sometimes I panic.' It came over her like waves, drowning her. 'And all sorts of silly ideas go rushing through my mind.'

He was very solicitous, though a little heavy with it, not used to being tender. 'There are people who do tracing,' he suggested. 'If you're really worried.'

'I've tried that. Saved and saved, then spent every penny on a man who came up with nothing.'

Then Chris realised what she'd been trying to say all along. 'So you see Johnny as your last hope?' And said like that it did sound as though she was being very silly and childish.

She was defensive. 'He would tell me. Johnny would.'

'But of course he would.' He sounded surprised that she needed to say it.

'If you can rescue him.'

'I can't promise anything.'

'You're doing all you can. I know that. More than anyone else would.' She was aware that he was watching her questioningly. 'With somebody trying to stop — '

He cut in, laughing. 'I was perhaps exaggerating things.'

'Were you?' She glanced at him. 'Perhaps

not. Is Mr Grey doing something about this man?'

He hesitated. 'He says he is. Says he's waiting for the next move. What's the next move likely to be, when he's already taken shots at me with a rifle?'

'Shots?'

'You're not to worry, Laura. Grey's got it in hand. Promise me you'll go home. I could have been imagining things.'

But it was too late to say that. She said she would go home, just to stop him from worrying. In just a few minutes, she promised.

He left it at that, and after a minute or so he went away. She returned to the cliff top, but now her mind wasn't on the bridge. She couldn't prevent herself from looking round, searching for a glimpse of Den, and afraid of the decision she would have to face if she saw him. Grey was always in view. She was scared of catching his eye, in case he read what she was thinking.

So in the end she went back to the farm earlier than she had intended.

It was dark, had been for a long time. She knew at once that Den was home, because of the shadow in the barn that was the pick-up. But there was the relief in knowing that at least he was away from the cliff. She went in.

He was stripping and oiling a rifle on her scrubbed pine table.

She went at him in fury. 'You've got oil on my table!' she screamed at him, because she had to cover her sudden terror.

He laughed, and as she ran at him, nails going for his eyes, he lashed out with his hand and sent her flying across the room.

Then he calmly set about putting it together again.

13

Marson was half demented with worry. The concrete was in at all four corners, the cables welded to two embedded girders the other side of the river, and the diesel winch bases this side were ready for bolting on, when the concrete was set. On the surface, things were going fine. He stood and watched, believing that nobody could know that he was raging inside at the futility of it. The whole scheme was based on the availability of a crane which could bear the weight of the truck. If he was denied the Jones there could be no happy ending.

He paced and thought, and juggled with permutations of the possibilities, and it all came back to the Jones.

Grey came and stood next to him, staring out at the wagon and saying it was all going well.

'Oh . . . sure,' Marson said.

'Hear the weather forecast?'

'No.'

'The wind's easing up a bit, but they reckon on more rain.'

More rain meant less time. 'Got any more cheerful news?'

Grey glanced at him. 'How long?' he asked.

'How long what, for God's sake?'

'Before you get your cables rigged, and the whole thing suspended.'

'What time is it?' It was ten o'clock. 'Five hours,' he said. 'Four, perhaps. It depends on how well the concrete sets. How quick.'

'And then,' Grey suggested, 'it'll be safe to drop a team on there, and cut him out?'

He'd got something on his mind, Marson realised. It was clear that he hadn't been paying enough attention to Grey. He was eager, intense, as far as Marson could tell in that light. But his eyes were deeply sunken and dark, and he seemed to be fading away inside his uniform.

'What gave you that idea?' Marson asked him.

'Just a thought.'

Marson couldn't see what he was getting at. There was an undertone to it he didn't like. 'A team, you say?' He decided to squash it, there and then. 'It'd certainly need a team. Six men, perhaps. Even with the cables rigged it'll be tricky — delicate. I'm not having a team of my men on there, not in any circumstances.'

Grey looked past him, not particularly disturbed that the operation couldn't be speeded up.

'I've got to have the Jones,' Marson told him, trying to spread his desperation.

Then at last Grey turned to face him squarely. 'The point is, Marson — I've had instructions.' His voice was a grumble — Grey was never pleased to take instructions — yet there was something that suggested he might have found them to his taste. 'I'm to turn it back. As soon as it reaches the end of the footings, it'll be leaving private property, and the question of theft would then arise.'

Marson went straight at him. 'Once we get it on public roads, we'll need a police escort — '

'You didn't hear what I said. My understanding is that you've got no permission to use that crane. In effect, it'll be stolen when it leaves the footings. I'm going to have to stop it.'

'Going to *have* to?' Marson shouted, his temper going. 'You're the bloody superintendent around here. Can't you make your own decisions?'

'Sievewright's got some very influential connections,' Grey said stiffly.

'So we play with politics and petty restrictions, while there's a human being out there? We've got to do what's necessary, and argue about it afterwards.'

Grey grimaced. 'Shoot first, and argue later? All right for you.'

'It's you it's all right for,' Marson snapped. 'It's not all right for me.'

Then why did Marson get the impression that it suited Grey in some way? Maybe it satisfied his tight little orderly mind.

'And you'll be breaking the law, Marson,' Grey said, all gloomy self-satisfaction. 'The Jones crane isn't yours to order around.'

Incredible as it might seem, Marson realised that this was what Grey wanted — delay. As he stared at the superintendent in disbelief, he suddenly realised that Grey had said too much. A distant memory: a name, a reputation slotted together. Marson had an idea.

'So you do your duty,' he told Grey. 'If it gives you any satisfaction.'

He thought that struck home. Grey looked at him suspiciously, then stalked away.

Marson spent the next few minutes looking for Allison. Things had gone quiet. All the work that was possible to do had been done, and most of the men were resting. The news people had gone away and the locals had lost interest, now that there seemed to be a lack of positive action. He couldn't find Allison, so decided he must have gone home too. He went to his caravan, to think.

But Allison hadn't left, and it was at the caravan that he found Marson. He stood in the doorway with his eyes on Marson in mute apology.

'Come in and shut the door,' Marson said.

'You didn't give me a firm answer,' Allison reproved him gently.

This was no game for a man like Allison, with his life involved in words and their precise meanings, in theory. This was all too close to human life and suffering, and he couldn't handle it.

'I don't remember the question. Remind me.'

'How long now — before it's safe?'

Marson took him to the graph they had started, and which he had pinned to the wall. The slide of the bridge was plotted against time. This thing was going to be an acceleration; not an arithmetic progression but a logarithmic one. So that the graph was going to be an exponential curve, like the bell of a trumpet.

Marson explained it in detail. The curve had just begun to dip. Slip against time.

'When it goes vertical,' he explained carefully; patiently, 'then the cliff's gone. You can see, it's beginning to progress. The curve's indicating its line. I could develop it right now — and get an answer.' Marson showed him with a pencil.

'What time's that?' Allison asked.

'Twelve hours from now.' Marson said it with the dedicated confidence of the theorist.

'You're so certain.'

'With the weather as it is now. If it dries out, we'll get a few more hours. More rain and we'll have a few less.'

'And then the cliff will be safe?'

The man hadn't understood a word. 'No,' said Marson. 'At that time the cliff'll come down.'

Allison blinked. Sheer, blind weariness was blunting his thinking. He had always been proud of his clarity of mind, and was vexed with himself.

'It'll be safe when I've got the slings under it. Then the cliffs will stop sliding. And that's in about five hours.'

'Have I got your word for that?'

'Of course.'

Allison nodded. Marson had presented him with time, a luxury now in Allison's life. Time to make decisions; time to which he could put them off. He smiled wearily. 'Thank you.'

He turned to leave. 'Don't go,' Marson said quickly. 'I'm making coffee.'

'I'll get off home . . . some rest . . . '

'I need your advice.'

'Mine?' Allison sat, more from surprise than intention.

'If you're the Allison I'm thinking of. Haven't I heard your name somewhere before?'

'Chris, the doctor. He's a friend of mine. He might have mentioned me.'

'No, no. Years ago. When I was working at head office. Sevco.'

Frank was beginning to realise what Marson could have been getting at, but he had no idea why. 'It's possible.'

'You had something of a reputation, didn't you? They always said the same thing: that you could work your way out of any contract, find a way to make anything legal.'

'Now look here — '

'It was you, wasn't it? Frank Allison? Sievewright used to curse you every day.'

Despite Frank's attempts to feign outrage, Marson's words found their target with relative ease. Frank had been good at his job, and the pride he had taken in his work still remained, a memory made all the more glorious by the years that had passed. He had always fought for the underdog. The motorway campaign was the greatest challenge he had ever taken on, a fight that was all but hopeless. But he missed the victories. The times when he had got one over on

Sievewright and his ilk — the millionaire businessmen squeezing every last penny out of the smaller firms they used — were the times he had felt happiest. Whether forcing them to pay a fair fee or tightening a clause which they had exploited for years or even finding a loop-hole they would never have dreamed of, he had come to know them. He liked to think that his name still gave them sleepless nights.

Marson watched him closely. The faint flicker of a smile told him all he needed to know. He launched at once into a detailed explanation of the problems with the Jones: Sievewright's objections, Grey's obstructions, the distance it still had to travel and the time it would take. Frank listened carefully, mulling over every word.

'Sievewright hasn't changed then,' he said.

'Not one bit,' replied Marson.

'I'd never have expected him to care about the driver, but the publicity . . . can't he see how well he'd do out of the whole thing?'

'All he can see is failure.' Marson shook his head miserably. 'And he doesn't want Sevco to have anything to do with failure.'

'And you really think Grey has his own agenda?'

'I'm not sure. Maybe it is just that he has his hands tied by Sievewright. But he sounds to me like he's got more on his mind than orders.'

'But why on earth would he want to delay things?' Allison's tone was more of confusion than disbelief. 'I mean, he won't be able to arrest the driver if he's stuck on the bridge; and surely it's not in his interests — or anybody's for that matter — for the bridge to fall?'

'Don't ask me,' said Marson. 'He's a law unto himself.'

Frank gave a little smile, but Marson didn't hear the joke. Allison was forced to get to the point. 'So what do you want me to do?'

'Anything,' implored Marson, 'anything at all. Use every trick in the book. Anything and everything you can think of. Just get me the Jones.'

Allison thought for a moment. It seemed to Marson that he already had an idea.

'This Jones. If I remember rightly, Sieve-wright doesn't actually *own* it, does he?'

'As good as. He hires it. Says that he doesn't have to pay for the maintenance that way. I can't remember the firm . . . I think it begins with 's' . . . something like . . . '

' . . . Spofford's' Allison finished for him.

'That's it, Spofford's. That's quite a memory. But I don't see how it will help. Sievewright's got them wrapped around his

169

little finger. The firm's been using the Jones for God knows how many years. He's got some special kind of renewable contract, I'm sure. An option. They can't do anything without his say so.'

'Spofford's of Leicester,' Frank continued, as though Marson hadn't spoken at all. 'I used to represent them, now and again.'

Marson came alive. 'You used to what?'

'Represent them. Against Sevco, as often as not. They think of me quite fondly, as I recall.'

'Even so,' thought Marson out loud, 'if they renege on their contract, Sievewright'll have them in court before the Jones even gets here.'

'True enough,' Frank admitted. 'But you said a very important little word just then. 'Renewable.' That's exactly it: renewable. Sievewright keeps all his lenders on the same tight lease. Renewal every calendar month. That way he holds on to their machinery as long as he wants — they'll never find so constant a source with another contractor — but he can throw it straight back at them at a moment's notice.' Judging by his words, Marson would have expected a certain amount of disgust to be prevalent in Allison's tone, but instead there was a hint of pleasure, and it grew stronger all the time.

170

'And how does this help us?' asked Marson, predicatably.

'What is the time, Mr Marson?' smiled Allison.

Marson glanced at his watch. 'Half-past ten.'

'And the date?'

'The date?' repeated Marson incredulously. 'The thirtieth of September.'

'So there's still time.'

'Time?' Time, as far as Marson knew, was the one thing they didn't have.

'Time. To renew the contract for ourselves. We can hire the Jones. Starting from the first of October. Midnight.'

Marson was stunned. He reached for the first thing that entered his mind: 'But it would cost — '

'A phone call,' interrupted Allison. 'I told you, they think of me fondly.'

'What about Sievewright?'

'There'd be nothing he could do. If he really needs the Jones, he won't have time to find another one, especially when Spofford's offer him their services as soon as the rescue is complete. So Spofford's will lose only a day's rental; and they *will* appreciate the publicity.'

Marson noticed that the rescue he had hitherto thought of as impossible was now — in the hands of this enthusiastic lawyer — being referred to as though it were a certainty.

'And best of all,' Allison carried on, 'Sievewright has no recourse to the law. None whatsoever. Because we will have done absolutely nothing wrong.'

Marson felt he could see how the man had got his reputation. Frank, meanwhile, was taken with the beauty of his own idea. He seemed a different person: for the first time in years there was hope, more than hope, of something other than failure.

He smiled winningly at Marson. 'I'll get back to my office. I should be able to reach Jon Spofford at home. And he can fax me the documentation. You get some rest.' He headed off into the cold.

Rest, thought Marson. How can I rest? Already he could hear the wind tumbling round the caravan. He put his coat on again and went out to check the bridge. He found Tony sitting in the Land-rover.

'Tony? Can't you sleep?'

'Somebody's got to listen out.'

'Hear anything?'

'He groans and mutters,' Tony said. 'It gives me the creeps.'

'Then get out of there.' He did. Marson caught his shoulder as he turned away. 'The

Jones is on its way.'

Tony turned and walked away briskly, his shoulders squared.

'There's some coffee in my caravan,' Marson shouted after him.

But Tony didn't get to it. Before he was half-way there, Marson saw a small spark of red down in the shadowed cluster. Then it bloomed, and a sheet of flame ran up the end of his caravan.

He began to run towards it. The caravan went up in an explosion of fire when he was a hundred yards short.

14

There was no point, she knew, in fighting with him. No point, really, in arguing, because Den couldn't ever see any point but his own. But she tried. She stood over him at the table and said:

'So it *was* you. I might have guessed.'

He didn't even look up, just went on sliding bits of metal together. 'Didn't I say?' he asked. 'Didn't I just warn you?'

'But it's pointless.' She sat opposite to him, trying to hammer it in, and do it calmly. 'Johnny's not going to say anything, not even when they get him out of there. He wouldn't let you down.'

'They ain't gonna get him out.'

'If they do, he still won't say anything,' she insisted. 'Why should he? He didn't before.'

'He ain't gonna get the chance.'

She had to keep trying. 'What *could* he say, Den? Except that he was coming home.'

'To you?' he shouted, and he thumped the table. 'It was to me, you stupid bitch, with all that whisky.'

'But I've persuaded everybody that he was coming to me,' she told him wearily.

'Heard you at it.' And now he was sneering. He lifted his eyes and stared at her. ' 'Johnny, I love you.' All that twaddle. You did well, I'll give you that. Fooled everybody good and proper. Yes, they all reckon he was coming to you.'

She screamed at him because he'd made a mockery of it. 'Because I meant it!' she shouted into his face. 'Because I'm doing everything I can to keep him alive. Lies, if you like, but it might help him.'

She had taken her eyes from his hands. Now he was waving a gleaming piece of metal under her nose.

'I'm telling yer — ' he started, but she'd had enough.

'But you go on with it, you crazy bastard,' she sobbed. 'Go on, get back to the bridge. They're waiting for you, all the police they can get their hands on. Did you think they wouldn't . . . ?'

He slashed at her. The metal winked with light and she threw herself back, the edge of it just catching her cheek like a touch of ice. Then she was over backwards with the chair flying, and Den was coming after her.

For a moment she thought he had blinded her. She was in a rage and a terror, and lashed out at him with her foot. She caught him on a kneecap and he howled and cursed, hopping about, so that she had a chance to get away. She scrambled to her feet and somehow got into the bedroom and locked the door, then wedged a chair under the door knob. Then he could hammer and shout himself hoarse as far as she was concerned.

She touched her cheek. At the sight of the blood on her fingers her temper flared. 'And you can clear out of this house!' she screamed. 'I'm going to get the police here.'

He must have moved away. 'You hear?' she shouted, thumping the door.

His voice startled her. He was speaking close to the panel. 'Hear you, Laura. Oh yeah, I hear you. But don't do anythin' rash, or you'll regret it.' He paused. She was holding her breath, and couldn't reply. 'Where d'you think I've been all day?' he breathed. 'Not all day to get this gun, sweetheart. I've been fixing things with some of me mates, and they phoned me. They've got Harry, Laura. Snatched him. So — watch your step.'

'I don't believe you,' she whispered, telling herself that she didn't, but he heard.

'Please yourself,' he said calmly, then she heard him walking away from the door, and she stood with her back to it, both hands pressed to her lips.

She was still there when she heard the pick-up start again. When its engine note faded she threw herself on the bed.

Her bedroom window faced directly over the valley. She was lying in the dark, wide awake and exhausted, when she noticed the rise and fall of the red light reflected on the rear wall. She got up, and could see the fire clearly.

'Now what's he done?' she asked herself emptily, and hoped he'd been arrested. Then she realised what this could mean to her. 'I don't believe him,' she whispered.

15

Marson's caravan was a smouldering wreck, with the red shape of a fire wagon sitting behind it. Men were wandering around and poking about. The rain had suddenly become as heavy as before and dampened down the few plumes of smoke which rose here and there. Marson himself was ranting at Grey.

'What's going on?' he shouted. 'This was deliberate, whatever you say. I'd only just left it. Someone came in here and turned the gas on. That makes two: first the ratchet, now this.'

Grey shrugged his shoulders. It was one thing to have explained his thinking to the doctor. Marson was a different proposition altogether. 'Somebody doesn't like what you're doing,' he muttered unhelpfully.

The useless mixture of curtness and ambiguity enraged Marson. He turned to the shadows. 'Nothing but opposition. Everywhere.' He swivelled back to Grey. 'Next you'll be telling me that *you've* got a nice little place down in the valley.'

'You can't bulldoze your way through the law, Marson.'

Marson sunk his head. He knew there was no point in rising to Grey's challenge here and now. Grey seemed to want delay. He seemed not to care whether Johnny lived or died, as long as he stayed out there. There was only one way to get back at Grey: Marson would have to rescue Johnny.

He turned to look for Jeff, just as Jeff approached him. 'Jeff. The fire destroyed all the predictions we'd made, and anyway the rain's much heavier now. I want you to go back to your caravan and draw up some new graphs. Until the cables are tightened and those slings are in place, we're going to need all the information we can get our hands on.'

Jeff nodded solemnly. 'That's what I wanted to talk to you about.'

'How's the concrete? Is it ready?'

Jeff hesitated. 'I'd like to leave it a little longer — '

'You'd like to?'

'We might have to.'

'Couldn't we just try the cables? The concrete should be able to take them by now. Surely?'

Jeff paused to consider. The operation had been planned in several stages. To begin with, they had constructed four concrete beds, two at the top of each cliff, set well back from the cracks. On the east side, girders had been

179

welded to the ends of the cables and buried in the concrete. The slings had been fastened over the cables and under the bridge, and the Kato had then taken the other ends over to the west side where they were weighed down, waiting slackly. When the concrete was ready, they would take up the slack with the winches and gradually support the weight of the bridge, the wagon, the lot. The cables themselves were two-inch steel-stranded. Though their weight was little compared to the tension which the concrete beds would eventually take, it was essential that all four beds set properly before the ends were threaded through the diesel winches, themselves fixed in the concrete on the other side.

'No.' Jeff shook his head. 'Not yet. Maybe in an hour or so. Look, if we put too much strain on the concrete before it's ready, it could ruin our chances altogether. You know that as well as I do. And this rain — '

'The heavier the rain, the less time we have. We need to buy some time.'

Jeff rubbed his chin demonstratively. 'I've been thinking. The Kato's not doing anything right now, and Tony's restless. We could send it round the other side and use it to give the trailer a little support. We wouldn't even try to lift it, just take some of the strain off the bridge.' He looked hopeful.

'You think it will help?' asked Marson, unconvinced.

'It can't hurt to try,' said Jeff, keen to be proved right.

Marson nodded, but without conviction. He knew the measure would probably make little difference, and he had serious reservations. Every alteration to so delicately balanced a situation was bound to have unforeseeable repercussions. There was no such thing as an action which couldn't hurt. But the cliffs were slipping. The Kato was now idle, and it would be at least an hour before they could move on to the next stage of the plan.

'You'd need to get some kind of cable under the trailer,' reasoned Marson.

'We could do that,' Jeff replied. 'Me and Tony. It wouldn't be a problem.'

'Okay. If you know what you're doing, you go ahead.'

Jeff smiled briefly, apparently with relief. He, too, hated having to do nothing. But this, he realised, was the first moment that Marson had trusted him, had trusted any of them. And to Jeff, it made success suddenly feel within their reach. He headed straight for Tony, who was now loitering beside the Kato. Marson watched as the change in Tony's stance spoke as clearly as any number of words. He began to turn towards Grey, to see how much of the conversation with Jeff he had understood; to see if the superintendent had noticed the more subtle changes in mood, the growing hope. And then, from nowhere, a boy was shouting in his ear:

'You're wanted, Mr Marson. Ray Foster. He says it's urgent.'

Marson grunted an acknowledgement and pushed Grey to one side. He recognised the young lad as one of his team, an apprentice, but the name escaped him. He ran after him to the radio shack. Ray Foster was talking earnestly into the microphone, as if comforting a child:

'It's okay, Marty. It's all right.' He looked up and nodded a greeting to Marson. 'Not a word of sense.'

Marson took the mike. Marty was cursing his head off. Marson had difficulty in slowing him down. Then at last he was coherent.

'Got to the end,' he said, 'the end of the footings, and there was a roadblock. Police cars, they were. Said I couldn't go onto the road. Mr Marson, you just give me the word — '

'Calm down, Marty. Calm down.' Marson managed to keep his voice under control, but all he could think of was Grey. An old policeman with a hidden agenda, answerable to no one. 'Wait with the Jones, and do nothing.'

'Gimme the word,' raved Marty, oblivious to Marson's efforts, 'and I'll plough through that lot — '

'I'll be along, Marty. Believe me, It's damned important for you just to wait.'

'For Christ's sake!'

'Marty! Are you listening to me? You have to wait.'

A pause. 'How long?'

'An hour. Maybe two.'

'Maybe two! I'm still ten miles away! If I wait two hours, I won't get to the bridge for at least another four.'

'Just wait and rest. For this job you'll need to be fresh. I'm warning you. It's bad here.'

Marty was quiet. As Marson had hoped, he was more responsive to requests which were expressed in terms of his value. 'Just wait, you say?'

'Just wait. Wait for me.'

'But what about the police?'

'They won't try to touch you unless you leave the footings. They have no right.'

'And you'll be along in an hour?'

'That's right, Marty. I'll be along. I promise.' There was no sound from Marty. Marson handed the mike back to Foster.

'What's going on, Colin?' Foster asked.

183

Marson tried to be brief. 'Sievewright's withholding the Jones, and Grey seems only too happy to help.'

'But — '

'It's okay, I'm sorting it.'

'You're sorting it? How?'

'There's no time to explain.'

Marson dashed out of the shack as quickly as he had entered. He had to find Allison.

16

Marson hadn't fully visualised what Jeff had had in mind. It was easy enough to say that they could take some of the load off the trailer by using the Kato, with a cable under the back of the wagon's load. But that cable would have to be under the trailer itself, not under the bridge; and at the same time it would have to avoid contact not only with the main support cables — which were yet to be brought into play — but also with Prescott's chains, which were still taking their share of the weight. As Marson continued to scour the area for Allison, Jeff was busy trying his plan the only way there was.

It had taken Tony a quarter of an hour to take the Kato round to the other side of the river and position it in the cutting, just before the rocky outcrop. Jeff meanwhile had seated himself on the chairlift and was now hanging halfway across the river, with a long pole in his hands. Cropper was hovering a little higher up on the other side of the wagon, one foot in the Kato's hook, dangling a loop of cable. Jeff was reaching under the trailer for the loop, nearly overbalancing every time he extended the pole. Backwards and forwards, the loop swinging, the chairlift pitching. The rain was heavy enough to make the pole slippery, and to disturb Jeff's concentration. He was struggling to see what he was doing, and Cropper found a new level of patience with every swing.

From the roadway, Chris was watching breathlessly. The fear he had felt while he was out on the chairlift had in no way hardened him to the thought of being suspended between those cliffs. He had no idea what they were trying to achieve, but seeing those two men playing peekaboo on either side of the lorry made his insides churn. Chris had set his alarm for half-past ten, half an hour before the time when Johnny's drip needed replacing. After precious little sleep he had forced himself to crawl out of bed. Pausing only to curse the cat, he had climbed into his car with his eyes barely open. He had driven all the way from the safety of his home back up to the bridge, precisely so that he too could be left hanging out there, with a job to do and only a hundred feet of wind and rain between him and a raging river.

'Chris!'

He turned away from the action to see Marson stomping towards him. 'What's going on out there?' asked Chris. 'Shouldn't you be supervising that?' He threw his arm back towards the bridge.

Marson followed his gesture just in time to see Jeff catch hold of the loop. They had spent nearly ten full minutes swinging and snatching and missing, but now that Jeff was securing the cable under the trailer it seemed like they had taken no time at all. 'They know what they're doing,' Marson replied quietly. 'And I know what I have to do. I've been looking for you.'

'I thought you'd forget,' said Chris.

'Forget what?' Marson moved back a step.

'About the drip. It's time for me to go out there again.'

'No, no,' said Marson quickly. 'There might not be any need. I want you to tell me where Allison is.'

'What do you mean 'need'? His drip has run out. I have to fix him a new one, or at least get a look at him. Once you've got those slings working, the bridge will move, won't it? Then the chairlift will be too low, and he'll have to wait even longer for treatment. I have to go out there before then. And anyway, what the hell's it got to do with Frank?'

It had not yet ocurred to Marson that an adjustment would need to be made to the chairlift. For a moment, he was grateful to the doctor. But only for a moment. He had no time for this. He had to get the Jones moving again. He didn't trust Marty to do as he was told. And the sooner the Jones arrived, the sooner it would all be over — the sooner Johnny would be safe. 'Just tell me where he is. I'll explain everything.'

Chris stopped to think. 'I . . . I saw the light on in his office,' he started, 'a little while ago now — '

'Number?'

'What?'

'His phone number, man!' Marson shouted. 'Allison's office. Give me his number.'

As Chris reached into his pocket for his diary, Marson's eyes followed him, unaware that Jeff and Cropper were already back alongside the Kato, talking to Tony. All three were nodding. Tony's reach from the west side of the river would be reasonably short to the trailer — approximately forty feet. At that radius he could manage a lift of thirty tons before he ran on to overload. Tony climbed into the cab, the engine already running steadily. The loop of half-inch cable hung from the hook, swaying irregularly in the wind. Jeff was looking to him questioningly. Tony replied by sticking up his thumb.

'Okay,' said Jeff. 'Take her up, but gently. Just take the weight. There's no point trying to lift the whole thing. If you can get the rear wheels clear of the bridge, that'll take a few tons off the cliffs. But take it slowly.'

The diesel settled to a steady throb. The cable started to twitch. Then it went rigid round the trailer's frame. Jeff watched uneasily as the gap between wheels and wheel arches began to open. Over on the east side, Marson snatched the diary from Chris's hands and turned sharply away from the cliff. His course was set and his mind closed as he dashed off to the phone box to speak to Allison. He was oblivious to the sounds which made even Chris turn at once to face the river. The bridge gave a groan. The main cables were whining in protest, when they should have been sighing with relief.

'Steady!' cried Jeff. 'Steady now.'

The overload hooter cut in. Jeff could not understand it. There was no way the Kato could have thirty tons on. He waved his arms at Tony in a frantic gesture. The engine died, the boom eased, the hooter stopped.

'I don't believe it,' said Tony. 'It doesn't make sense.' The indicator pointed to thirty-two tons, and the trailer hadn't lifted an inch. 'How can it not have moved? I know what this thing's capable of . . . '

'Me too,' agreed Jeff.

Even Cropper was nodding. 'There must

be something else.'

Jeff looked at the dials. 'Maybe there is,' he began slowly. 'What if we tried it with the boom further out?'

'We'd just get even less lift,' Tony came back quickly. 'You know that. The further out the boom, the less lift I can get. Try to lift more vertically and we'd get nowhere.'

'We're also trying to pull it backwards, aren't we? To slide it?'

'If you can't manage a perpendicular lift, then some of the forces pull horizontally.' Tony was mumbling impatiently. 'Of course they do.'

'But if the driver has locked the wagon's brakes, then we're trying to pull against that as well.'

Tony and Cropper looked on, reluctant to admit that that could be the problem. They had lifted many things in their time, and Tony's explanation had worked for everything. If a vertical lift is impossible, then you lift at an angle. The shorter radius means a greater capacity, and this makes the lift possible; that was the way it worked. But neither of them had ever tried to lift a wagon, less still a wagon with its brakes locked.

Jeff waited for the silence to end. But there was no response. 'Try it again,' he said at last, the lack of dissension convincing him of his authority. 'Try it with the boom further out. Try a vertical lift. Dead vertical.'

Tony turned back to the controls. He extended the boom, still saying nothing. When the hook was directly over the cable's point of contact with the trailer, Jeff gave him a nod and the engine again began to throb. Again the cable tightened. The load began to lift a little sooner this time, but barely more discernibly. They were still unsure whether the wheels had been lifted even a millimetre from the surface when the hooter cut in again. Jeff made a gesture, and Tony eased the throttle until the hooter cut off. The indicator was pointing to nineteen tons.

'Leave it at that,' said Jeff.

He had been right about the brakes, but his disappointment was obvious. The fraction of strain they had taken off the cliffs was almost negligible, yet the sound of whining metal which now filled the air convinced them of only one thing: they had added to the uncertainty. Who knew what loads and forces they had disturbed, or what effect these changes would make? And worse still, the Kato was now stuck. Even the slightest movement now seemed too risky. Tony realised before anyone else that his role in the entire operation was effectively at an end. He accepted it bravely.

'A good try,' he conceded.

Jeff gave an uncharacteristic snarl and moved away from the Kato. Cropper followed him, but Tony sat still in the Kato, pointlessly. They had achieved nothing. When Jeff and Cropper got back to the base on the east side, Marson was waiting for them outside Jeff's caravan.

'The Kato's stuck,' said Jeff, by way of greeting.

'So I see,' said Marson.

Jeff stood head down, like a schoolboy, owning up to a crime which the headmaster already knew about. 'It hasn't made much difference,' he said, after a while.

'So I hear,' said Marson. 'It was a good try. I've been having a few problems myself.'

'Problems?'

The plan to use the Kato had drawn Jeff's attention away from the rest of the operation. Marson had yet to tell him about Sievewright's attempts to keep the Jones from them, and about Grey's efforts to help him. Jeff hadn't needed to be told to know that there was something wrong; but for the last hour or so he had forgotten even that.

'With the Jones,' explained Marson. 'Sieve-wright's playing silly buggers, so we have to hire it ourselves, for the day.'

'We what?' This was beyond even Jeff's suspicions.

'It's okay. Frank Allison's sorting it for us. He says that he's run into a few small problems, but he'll be along as soon as a fax comes through from Spofford's.'

'We can't do anything without the Jones,' muttered Jeff.

'No. We can't do *everything* without the Jones,' Marson replied. 'That doesn't mean we can't do something.'

'What are you trying to say?'

'I'm not sitting here, twiddling my thumbs, waiting for a piece of paper. The rain's still falling, the cliffs are still slipping. We have to do everything we can to slow them down. You said an hour; it's been nearly an hour. Let's try the cables.'

'But if we wait a little longer — '

'Now. We'll inspect the concrete again before we try the slings, but we'll run the cables out now. Cropper, you know what to do.'

Cropper looked at Jeff. Jeff shrugged. Cropper looked back at Marson. Cropper shrugged.

'Okay, boss.'

It was tricky, and slower than Marson had

imagined, more of a fiddly process than the big jobs they had been tackling so far. Cropper used light lifting equipment to get the ends of the cables up to the height of the tripods. Then they used lengths of half-inch cable as lead-ins. Despite all the calculations he had made, Marson felt his heart stop several times. He had had to take a shot at guessing the weight of the bridge and the chains and the wagon, and had resolved it all into a load diagram, with all the stresses in all the planes. The whole thing was based on guesses — good guesses perhaps, but guesses nonetheless — and so the whole operation was beset with doubt. Every now and again he would feel sure that he had worked out the distances and the lengths incorrectly for the cables to slope down at a reasonable angle, and at each of these moments, Cropper was little help, occasionally mumbling that the tripods should have been taller, the slings longer. But once they had take-up on the winches and the slings began to draw nearer the bridge, the doubts grew more scarce. Jeff left Marson's side for a few minutes, then returned to confirm that the concrete was fine, but they had to wait — maybe as much as another hour — before they tried to support the bridge. Marson knew that that was where all the real difficulties would lie, but the small success with the cables helped him immensely. The rescue was beginning to seem more possible than ever before. All they had to do now was wait.

17

She had stood and watched from her window until the flickering red glow died, and then she realised that she knew where Den was, at least for a time, and spent the best part of the next hour in a frantic search for his gun. But he must have had it with him, she realised.

He came in hours after she'd given up hope, his nose red and swollen, and he demanded food. She cooked for him, not speaking, not really looking at him. She was surprised that he was able to sit at the table, his nerves were on such an edge. It didn't have to mean he'd achieved much. If he'd managed to do any real harm, he'd have been boasting about it.

No — it was the fire. He'd lit it and watched it, and some of the heat had seeped into his veins. She had seen him like it before, and knew it would fade, probably into sullen fury. So she put food into him. This time his tension faded into a yawn, and he couldn't even find the energy to snarl at her.

Then he dragged himself into his room.

She had to give him time to get to sleep. She sat at the table for half an hour, and waited. Then she opened his door quietly and peeped in. He hadn't even taken his boots off, and was snoring, flat on his back.

She was out to the pick-up in seconds. It was the only place the gun could be, and this was an ideal chance to get it and break it in some way.

But she couldn't see it there, either. Oh, he was clever. Cunning more like. He'd known what she would do, so he'd put it somewhere else before coming into the house.

He'd left the pick-up in the barn, where he kept the tellies from his last job. She realised, then, that the ones he'd taken away had been swapped for the gun. But it could've been anywhere. There was no end of hay still around in scattered piles, but it wasn't in any of them. She couldn't find it, and was almost sobbing with frustration when her dad came in, giving her quite a start.

Her father always moved quietly, and didn't usually say much. He just stood in the half-open doorway. 'Laura?' he said.

She stood, arms away from her sides, and said: 'I'm looking for his gun.'

'I don't want you to find it,' he said, shaking his head.

It was the way he'd said it: her father had never understood violence, but she realised that he was thinking of it now.

'Why?' she demanded. 'Dad . . . you know where it is.'

'If I tell you, you'll kill him.' He sounded so calm about it.

She tried to explain that she'd got something different in mind for the gun. 'That wasn't why — ' she began.

But he cut in: 'I can read you like a book.' He'd never read a book in his life.

But maybe he could, because she'd been trying not to think about killing, and it must have shown. 'It's not that!' she cried. 'I only wanted to put it out of action. That's all.' She wasn't sure what she wanted, except that it was something to harm Den, to hurt him.

He smiled, his sweet old smile. 'I'd have killed him myself, if it hadn't been for little Harry.'

'You're talking crazy, Dad,' she told him, worried by the smile. 'You keep out of it. Tell me where he hides it.'

He sucked in his lips, his teeth clicking. 'It's under the seats of the pick-up.'

She ran across to it. What her father had said was giving her frightening ideas. But she didn't dare to dwell on them, because she didn't dare to assume that Den was lying.

It was where he'd said. She couldn't see how she'd missed it before. She drew it out. It seemed heavy, but not unwieldy. Her heart was hammering, and for a few seconds the gun was just a blur in her hands.

From behind her, her father said quietly: 'But we don't need Den.'

She turned with it, and took two paces towards the barn door. The old man was watching her. They were going to kill Den. That was clearly the best thing to do. And afterwards ... There was a chilling void afterwards. Her father nodded. Then Den was there, in the doorway, his head tilted forwards.

'Give it to me,' he said. His voice was blurred with sleep.

She pointed it at him, the stock under her arm. Suddenly it felt awkward. He laughed at her. 'You don't think I'd leave one up the spout,' he said.

That didn't mean anything to her. She raised the stock to her shoulder. He was in the sights, and coming at her, his laugh gone but his lips twisted. But when she pulled the trigger all her determination seemed to melt away, and she moved the barrel as the shot rang out.

A thin line of red appeared along his neck, but he carried on walking forward as though he felt nothing. He took the gun from her hands and brought the stock round and hard down on her shoulder, his teeth showing because he enjoyed it. She thought she cried out, and she went down into the hay, half fainting, and saw that he'd raised the gun high and was aiming the stock at her face. She rolled free, and again it caught her on the shoulder. But she didn't dare to give way to the pain, and had to struggle away and somehow get to her feet. Then she scrambled for the doorway, and heard the hard, metallic sound as he re-loaded it. When the first shot rang out she was running, right arm held across her chest, running down the mud of the lane, slipping and sliding and sobbing. There was another shot, and another. She thought he must be firing in the air.

She stopped and turned. There was no point. She stared back at him, waiting for him to shoot her, but he was standing there laughing viciously. Her dad was standing behind him in the doorway, bending over slightly. He had the silhouette of a beaten man. She was determined not to give in so easily.

She turned slowly and walked away from him, striding down the drive, her steps beating out a measured defiance. She was heading for Prescott's Bridge. She didn't look back once, but she could tell that Den was not coming after her. There were no footsteps other than her own, and this alone felt like a victory. Her shoulder began to throb. She'd taken beatings from him before, and she was no stranger to pain, but pain had never been this bad. It grew like a ball of fire, sparking suddenly as she moved out of the light from the farm, taking on a life of its own once she was in darkness. She tried to concentrate on the rain which drove against her face, on the feel of her matted hair along the back of her neck, but the pain engulfed her. It spread from her shoulder to the side of her head, down her arm, through her body. She could think of nothing but death; she was sure the pain would kill her. It never eased, only grew. She would die, because death would be a relief. Still, she forced one foot in front of the other, knowing that it was only her momentum which kept her going.

Within a few minutes, Den was beside her, trundling along at her own steady pace in the Mini. His window was open and he was leaning out, laughing.

'Don't be a fool, Laura,' he mocked. 'I'll take you back.'

She kept her head still, eyes front.

'Get in the car.'

Her course was fixed.

'Go on,' he laughed, 'get in the car. I'll take you back to your dad.'

Laura froze. The mention of her father

stopped her dead in her tracks. She looked across. Den was still smiling. She saw the gun his lap as he drew the car to a halt alongside her. All at once the pain overwhelmed her. She dropped to her knees, clutching her shoulder in agony, so far from being able to think that she could not even hate herself for her weakness. She reached out for the car door. Den gave a short laugh, and accelerated away, leaving her to fall flat in the tracks he left behind. He drove back home, where he slept briefly and fitfully, with the gun in his arms like a teddy bear.

Laura watched the Mini disappear, and cried and cried. It was many minutes before she dragged herself to her feet and stumbled towards the cliffs. When she arrived, the scene seemed to her altogether different. There was a new, tense atmosphere, unlike anything she had felt there so far. The news seemed to have gone round that something critical was afoot. The crowd, which had dwindled earlier in the evening, had now grown to over a hundred locals, kept back from the cliff with some difficulty by only a dozen or so policeman. The TV cameramen had brought their van up with the camera on its roof, to give themselves a good view of the bridge. Two other men had smaller versions resting on their shoulders. An interviewer was in amongst the crowd, attempting to extract angry soundbites by sticking a microphone into the faces of members of the public, prompting them to doubt the competence of those in charge, inciting them to make their presence felt.

One woman broke free of the inadequate police cordon and ran to the loudhailer. The feedback pierced the noise as she began to scream: 'They've been lying to us. All along they've been lying. I've seen their boss. He doesn't know what he's doing. No more than my ol' feller would. No more than me. He told us it'd be safe.' She gestured frantically behind her. 'Does this sound safe to you?' A charged hush had greeted her words. Everyone could feel the vibrations through the soles of their feet. They could hear the rock groan. 'They're playing, that's all. Like little boys with Lego. But their playing with our homes, our families, our *lives*!'

The woman's speech was having a palpable effect. At first, the crowd had quietened to hear her, and everyone on this side of the river had stopped and listened. Everyone except Marson. He saw the danger at once and began running towards her. Jeff took off immediately after him, but couldn't keep up. Marson stole up behind her and wrenched the loudhailer from her grasp, pushing her to the ground. The mob surged, apparently ready to burst forward and sweep him from the cliff. Their faces were distorted as they waved and pointed, their mouths open and their eyes wide.

'Don't listen to this mad woman!' Marson yelled into the loudhailer. Jeff drew up beside him, willing him to choose his words more carefully. Lower Prescott was a small town. Most of these inhabitants knew each other; at least half would know the woman. If Marson carried on as tactlessly, they would have a riot on their hands. 'We'll save your homes, your land,' he continued. 'We know what we're doing.' He turned to face Jeff. Though he wasn't speaking into the loudhailer, he left it on deliberately, wanting the crowd to hear him. 'Jeff, let's take up the slack.'

Jeff had to stop and think. He wasn't sure what Marson was referring to.

'It's ready, Jeff. The concrete's ready. It's time to support the bridge.'

'But, Colin — '

'It's now or never. If we don't do something now, this lot'll ruin everything. They'll act first and think later. It's up to us to keep that driver alive.'

Jeff had no option but to give in. As he stepped back, out of Marson's way, he prayed that the concrete would not do the same.

Marson headed across to the diesel winches; Jeff followed loyally. Cropper had got both winches chugging away, keeping them ready for whenever the time was said to be right. Marson took one, Jeff the other. They stood either side of the cutting. He held the loudhailer down at his side — the winches at full blast would be deafening. All eyes were on him. His were on the bridge.

It was now swaying gently, a movement of no more than a foot, taking several seconds each way. The tripods looked firm and well placed, sufficiently back from the edge. The pulleys at their apexes were well greased. It occurred to both Marson and Jeff that the main cables were too level. Cropper saw the moment of hesitation, the look that passed between them, and felt that he had been right. But it was done; whether or not it could have been better, there was no turning back now. Chris sat in the Land-rover; listening to Johnny's sounds over the radio was as close as he could get to reaching his patient. Marson looked around. His mouth was dry. Jeff lifted a hand to his throttle. Marson nodded.

'Okay, Jeff?' he spoke into the loudhailer.

Jeff waved and shouted something out, at the same time returning his nod.

'Right,' called Marson. 'On the count of

three — and dead slow. One ... two ... three ... '

In unison, they advanced the throttles. The two diesels took on a solid, more throaty sound. The winches slowly revolved and over the pulleys the cables gradually tensed. Then the slings tightened as the weight came on, and the tripods bit into the rock. Jeff thought he could feel the concrete crumbling, but told himself that all he could feel was fear. The exhausts thudded. Marson shouted out a command. Only Jeff could hear him, but he waved an acknowledgement and eased off a little. Marson's side of the bridge had the lower dip, so he had to take in more cable. He advanced his throttle a fraction.

There was a cracking sound from the bridge, and a six-foot length of parapet flew high into the air. The rain battered it back down, and the wind hurled it towards the river. The winch beside Marson howled and the cable chattered as it dug down onto itself. The winding slowed considerably as the winches felt the load. The exhausts threw out separate belches of thick black smoke. Sweat was trickling down his back.

The bridge moved again, more discernibly. More metal flew away, hanger bars flicked and writhed. All eyes were turned now to the bridge. The movement was most easily observed in the angle of the lorry's slant. The wagon rose steadily — an inch, two inches. Everything was fine. Everything but Marson's nerves. The rock vibrated beneath him. He waved to Jeff and called out: 'Hold it!'

They locked on the brakes. There was a sigh from the crowd. Marson went forward to have a look. It needed calculation. He had 167 tons of breaking strain on each cable, but as the angle of the fall shallowed, the load on them increased. They would have to take it further. Not to take all the load, but more of it. Most of it.

Chris, in the Land-rover, had his hands covering his face.

Marson turned back to Jeff. 'Again,' he called through the loudhailer. 'And slowly.'

Jeff wanted them to stop there. He wanted to discuss the decision — such an enormous decision — but Marson wouldn't even have been able to hear him. And because there was no chance of being heard, Jeff lowered his head and agreed.

Marson was taking in two inches to Jeff's one, trying to lift the wagon level. The cab lifted, an inch at a time, gradually levelling off. But so slowly. No — it was not right. Marson felt old and battered, his legs shaking. There was a confluence of forces out there, something impossible to have calculated or compensated for. Something was restraining it.

The cables were now down to a mere creep. The bridge wasn't moving any more, the cables taking it all, the whine from them rising in pitch until it was a shriek. Jeff was standing as though part of the rock, just as grey. Marson held on, forcing it, pushing it. It was just possible to detect the winch drum moving. But the bridge was not, and they had to have more. He was whispering to it, as though it was a child. It cried out, like a creature in pain. No! Suddenly Marson knew it. He felt the knowledge run through him.

There was a crack across the water, and a booming shudder. The wagon lurched and the cables whipped, and for one moment Marson thought they'd lost it, lost everything.

18

A piercing scream came from the Land-rover, from the radio — from Johnny — and then it died to a whisper. He was still alive, but his pain was increasing all the time. The bridge settled. The cab was now leaning no more than five degrees, and they had it.

'Hold it right there,' Marson croaked into the loudhailer.

They locked on. Beneath his feet he felt the gentle movement. He did not look down, refusing to trust his battered senses. The rain poured from his face. He made cutting gestures, and the diesels sobbed to a halt. There was a muttering groan from the crowd. For a moment, he thought it could have been applause; but he knew that even they would realise that this had been nothing to applaud. The idea of attempting to support the load had sounded so good, so simple. But that was its real failing. Nothing in this situation was as simple as Marson had tried to make it. He reached for a cigarette and slowly began to light it, using the cupping of a match to cover his real action. He was looking down at the rock. He felt the camera on him, and all the assembled eyes, the crowd waiting. His toe was resting on the rock surface in line with the winch.

There was a new crack.

The concrete hadn't failed. It was like rock — better than rock. But there was a new crack. They had not succeeded in removing the danger from the cliffs. It was still there, with the same load torturing the same argillaceous rock, but more of it, further back.

Cropper had been correct, in one way. The tripods should have been taller. The main cables were too level. Marson had to take them in too much, which meant that their angle was too shallow. This had put the strain on them very close to their breaking point. The pulleys had redirected this load so that it was nearly horizontal. The bridge was now trying to pull the cliffs in towards the river. And so a new crack had appeared, ten yards further in than the original crack on the east side, and heaven only knew how deep. Where there had been hundreds of tons of rock poised to fill the river and flood Lower Prescott, there were now thousands. What little time the operation might have bought was meaningless. All Marson had achieved was to make the likelihood of disaster a near certainty.

He felt desperate. Against opposition from every corner, from every human force and seemingly from every divine agent, he had managed to put together a decent-sounding plan, and to see it carried out exactly as he had envisaged. And he had only made things worse. The fault lay with him, buried within his character, as sure and as dangerous as the fault deep within the cliffs beneath him. The last remaining hope was to pick the truck off the bridge. But even if the Jones had not been tied up in red tape back at the footings, this would only slow the slide, not stop it altogether. The rain was falling as heavily as ever. With or without the Jones, Lower Prescott would drown.

For the first time, Marson wanted to fall to his knees and beat the cliff with his fists. To yell out every last ache of frustration and responsibility and despair, and to use his own bare hands to precipitate the inevitable calamity. To show that he alone was in control, by bringing the whole thing down with his own brute strength. Instead, he lifted his head passively. The man with the microphone was approaching. The cameras were closing in.

'Is it done?' the man asked. Marson looked back at his cigarette. There was no point in lying. There was no way he could tell the truth. He remained silent.

'Is it done?' repeated the man.

'The driver's still out there.' Marson answered like a politician. 'We won't have finished until he's here, safe, with us. For that, I need another crane. Nothing is done until that crane arrives.'

'But these people,' the interviewer persisted, 'are their homes safe? Would you guarantee their livelihoods?'

'Would anyone?' smiled Marson, relieved to have so easy an escape.

The crowd were less sure than ever. They understood even less, but felt less in a position to make demands than a few minutes earlier. They had been made promises, yet they had no way of knowing whether or not these promises were being kept.

As Marson walked away with Jeff, pushing past angry questions and uneasy expressions to get back to the caravans, Chris joined them as if from nowhere.

'Did you hear him scream?' he asked.

'Who didn't?' Questions, he thought to himself, are often the best answers.

'I've got to get out there again. His position will have changed. He may even be free of the wreck.'

'No,' said Jeff quietly, 'he won't be free.'

'Look!' Chris was starting to shout. 'You've

got to get me out there!'

'Please, Chris,' said Marson insipidly. 'Please. Not now.'

Marson recognised that the doctor's nerves were as frayed as anyone's. For nearly two days now, he had lived with the sheer terror of having to risk his life to save another. And worse than the fear was the uncertainty; not only of his patient's condition, but of access to that patient. He never knew when he would be able to get across, or what he would be able to do when he got there. He hated every crossing with all his body and soul. And yet, more selflessly than anyone else in the operation, he insisted on going out, again and again.

Marson turned to appease him, and to show more appreciation of his position than he had done before. But as he began to speak, all three men stopped walking and looked ahead. A figure was running towards them, waving its arms over its head, shouting out.

'Marson!' The cry grew more distinct as the man drew nearer. He was waving a piece of paper. 'Mr Marson!'

'Frank?' said Chris, the most surprised of the three.

'I have it, Mr Marson. I have the Jones!'

Marson began to run towards him. 'You've got it?' he gasped.

Frank Allison was seriously short of breath by the time the two men reached each other. As his face grew first pale, then beetroot, Chris thought he might have to go back for his bag. 'One Jones model 971C. It's yours, Mr Marson. This piece of paper — complete with the signature of Mr Spofford himself — is all the authority you need.'

Jeff stood back, stunned. Chris looked on, confused.

'Now then,' said Frank, still struggling to breathe, 'all that's left is for you to save our town.'

'I'll do what I can,' smiled Marson. 'Jeff. You get Cropper and sort out the chairlift for Chris. I'll be back as soon as I can. I want you to make all the arrangements necessary to bring the Jones as close as we can.'

'Will do, boss,' nodded Jeff.

'You can't leave now,' started Chris.

'I'm going to meet Marty.' Marson spoke with sudden, genuine confidence. 'I'm going to get the Jones, and then we're going to pick that truck right off that bridge. Jeff will look after things until I get back.' He smiled sincerely, for the first time since the police sergeant had woken him on Tuesday morning, and ran off towards the cluster of vehicles near Jeff's caravan. He jumped into the nearest van and headed for the footings.

19

The rain had eased slightly. The wind had died. The bridge sat there, wrapped in a binding of cable, more upright and more stable, and so motionless that there seemed to be no reason for the shuddering. But still the rock was transmitting it. Jeff, Chris and Cropper stood at the cliff top looking out, assessing the course of their next action. All three of them could feel it. They knew that there was something wrong. Jeff knew that it was something serious. But all three knew better than to mention it.

Cropper squared his shoulders and cast his eyes scornfully over the bridge. When he spoke, his voice was relaxed. 'That chairlift'll be too low, now. Its tripods need lifting five or six feet.'

'Good,' agreed Jeff. 'Work out how to do it, and get Tony out of that Kato and over here. He can give you a hand.'

'I'll need jacks, some more girders — '

'Don't tell me,' snapped Jeff. 'Time's short enough. Get the equipment you need, bring in the men you need, and get on with it.'

'But there's — '

'For Christ's sake, Cropper. What are you babbling about?'

Cropper shrunk back slightly. 'Have you looked out there recently? Closely. Down at the cab, I mean. It might have been the Kato. More likely it was the winches, though. Have a look.'

Cropper handed Jeff a pair of binoculars which he hardly needed. The problem wasn't that it was difficult to see out, nor that the object was particularly small. Cropper was right; no one had looked closely in the last few hours. They hadn't been paying enough attention to the details around the lorry itself.

'Oh shit,' murmured Jeff, passing the binoculars to Chris.

The three men stood silently as Chris looked out. No words were spoken, but both Jeff and Cropper knew that Chris had seen the problem for himself. They felt the sickening lurch which accompanied his realisation, the despair at facing yet another obstacle in what was beginning to seem an endless assault course. One of the sling cables lay tightly against the cab, crossing the foot-square observation hole to Johnny's foot. A hanger bar had come loose at some point during the changes which Marson had forced onto the equilibrium. It had fixed itself across the driver's window. There was now no way for Chris to get to him. No way to see him, no way to treat him — and certainly no way to replace his drip. The measures taken to support the bridge seemed to have prevented any useful action to look after Johnny.

'We may as well stop now,' said Jeff. 'There's nothing more you can do.'

'Nothing?' cried Chris, incredulous. 'There must be something. He's had no nourishment for hours. He's suffering from shock, exposure. He's losing blood. He must have lost hope long ago. I have to get to him.'

'Go home,' said Jeff quietly. 'Get some sleep. Come back in an hour or two and we might be picking him off the bridge. Unless . . . *until* we can bring him to you, there is nothing more for you to do here.'

'And if he's dead by then?' Chris was no longer capable of subtlety.

Jeff was used to dealing with blunt questions, and giving equally blunt answers. 'Then you'll have done your best. More than your best. But alone, on a chairlift, there's no way you can get past that hanger bar.'

'No,' interrupted Cropper, 'he can't. But who says he has to go alone?'

'What?' said Jeff.

'We've already had two people out on that chairlift, and the wind's died since then.

There's no reason why two can't go out again.'

'What are you saying?' Chris asked hopefully.

'The two of us could go across together. Me and you. I'll cut that bar, an' you can get at the driver.'

'No,' said Jeff, solemnly. 'There's no telling what stress that bar's taking. You saw what happened with the Kato. Cutting that could bring the whole lot down.'

'Come on,' said Cropper, sounding like a child. 'Be serious. How likely is that?'

'It's not about likelihood,' Jeff replied sternly. 'It's about risk, about possibility. And about danger.'

'And what about Johnny?' Chris spoke with the most gravity, and his words were telling. 'So there's a risk. Well, me and Cropper are willing to take that risk. If you try to stop us, you're not helping anyone, and you may well be killing that man out there. He's the one in danger, and who's he got to speak for him? If we can help him, we should.'

Jeff felt the weight of Chris's argument, was forced to share his burden. Marson would not have given in. Perhaps Marson should not have left at so critical a stage. Perhaps he should have sent Allison to get the Jones past the police. But perhaps was neither here nor there. Marson had gone, and the decision was Jeff's. Marson would not have given in, but Marson was often wrong. Marson had no idea how to manage his team. Management was about compromise. Jeff could not simply forbid so selfless an action. He would concede, and gain ground elsewhere.

'You'll both have safety lines,' he said firmly.

'Safety lines?' There was a look of horror on Cropper's face. But Jeff knew that his condition would be accepted. Cropper thought of wearing a lifeline as a precocious child thinks of having stabilisers on his bike: unnecessary, restrictive, and highly embarrassing. But he knew that Jeff would raise too much opposition unless he agreed to use them, and this was a small price to pay for the glory of saving a life. 'If it'll make you feel better,' he laughed.

'I'll go and get my bag,' said Chris.

Jeff watched them head off together before Cropper made for the tripods and Chris went to his car. They didn't speak a word.

★ ★ ★

Chris watched them re-rigging the safety lines. Tony had helped to raise the tripods and then returned to the Kato, leaving the rest of the operation to Cropper and Jeff. It seemed that he was happier doing nothing in his crane than doing something useful anywhere else. Cropper grunted with contempt as they slipped the loop of rope beneath his armpits. As before, Chris was quietly grateful, though this time the reassurance he felt was a thin impression of its former self. Jeff's words of warning about the delicate balance and the stresses in the bar were beginning to register. The rope would be no help at all if the bridge fell on them.

Two things were clear: that Chris was not going to reach Johnny without Cropper's assistance; and that he felt much more secure with Cropper beside him. Cropper clasped eighteen inches of brass cutting torch in his right hand, and held his red and black gas bottles down on his knees. Chris held on to his bag as though it contained life itself. They were swung out over the river.

The rain was now little more than a fine drizzle. The breeze was stiffening to a fair wind, but there was so far no sign that it was agitating the bridge, apart from a few metallic groans. With his heart recovering from the initial surge, Chris was beginning to feel mildly excited. He had, for the first time in a long time, begun to persuade himself that they at last had a chance of achieving something.

They stopped, gently swaying, beside the cab door. Chris signalled to be moved a little higher, anxious to get a better look at the prospects. The hanger bar was lying across the side of the cab. There was perhaps room for him to get a shoulder past it. He turned to see if Cropper was thinking along the same lines.

Cropper was making businesslike adjustments to his apparatus.

'What d'you think?' shouted Chris.

Cropper could only just hear him. 'I've got an idea,' he replied glibly.

'This is no time to have ideas — ' Chris yelled, but he could see that Cropper had had the idea a while ago. Whatever it was, it had been on his mind before he assented to wearing the harness, even before he had suggested that he and Chris go out together. The look of determination in his eyes made Chris fear for his life as never before.

'I can cut the door out,' said Cropper. 'The thickness of metal we got here — hell, I could cut round this door in under five minutes. Then we could get a good looksee at his foot. Or you could.'

Chris couldn't believe his ears. His life was entirely dependent on this huge, lumbering idiot. He wanted to scream, to get off that plank of wood at once. But then his fear for Johnny kicked in again, quelling his anger, numbing his instincts for self-preservation. 'And then you'd be able to cut the metal that's trapping his foot?'

'Don't see why not,' said Cropper, almost flippantly.

'But the metal would get hot, wouldn't it?' suggested Chris. 'Red hot?'

'Well, sure.' Cropper looked worried. 'But you can give him something, huh?'

Chris was looking serious, his lower lip jutting. 'Have you ever smelt burning human flesh, Cropper?'

Cropper had no response.

'Look,' shouted Chris, 'you tackle the hanger rod first. Then maybe I can get at him through the window.'

Cropper shook his head stubbornly. 'We can do it. You an' me.'

'The rod, Cropper. Let's see how he is.'

'I could leave the rod,' pleaded Cropper, 'and take the door out. You heard Jeff: we don't know what stress the rod's taking. The door's doing nothing, just getting in the way. I could take the door out, leave the rod. And then you could get at him.'

Chris was trying to be patient. The chairlift was beginning to react to the wind, swaying gently, making him feel giddy. 'But we'd have to leave him here then,' he replied tensely. 'Don't you see that? The rain hasn't stopped; the wind could pick up. We can't leave him with no cover. Please, Cropper. The hanger bar.'

'But Jeff said . . . ' Cropper's words trailed off. Chris had robbed Cropper of his grand design, the plan he had kept to himself which he was sure would save the day and make him a hero. Now Cropper was losing heart. He grunted and reached for his matches.

Jeff watched helplessly from the cliff as the torch caught with a pop. Two feet of orange smoky flame shot out. He turned the other valve on his torch and it roared into a blue cone. He got to his feet. He turned to Chris with a snarl of twisted defiance. Chris nodded: the bar, Cropper. Jeff sensed the threat, the tension that was ready to snap. He reached down for the loudhailer, put it to his mouth, ready to call out.

The flame bit in, spraying tiny red-hot globules of steel. The cone hissed.

The loudhailer cracked in: 'Cropper — '

But it was too late. The rod parted. The strain on it was released and it whipped back, catching Cropper across the chest. He gave a small weak cry and disappeared over the edge of the chair.

The chairlift pitched and Chris made a frantic grab for him. His fingers gripped only the lifeline, which burned across his palm. He was aware of a grating of metal from the bridge, but dared not glance back at it. He was flat on his chest, head over the guard rail. Cropper fell, then twisted, then stopped abruptly as the lifeline caught him. He hung, unconscious, head back and body arched, eight feet below Chris.

The loudhailer squawked: 'The torch! Chris, the torch!'

But the warning was too late. It had fallen, still roaring, on the chairlift, its flame pointing away from Chris but too close to one of the support ropes. As he watched, his hand moving towards it in agonising slow-motion, the rope smoked and flared, and parted. One corner of the chair tilted, and the torch slid over the edge, trailing its rubber hoses behind it. The gas bottles were rolling. Chris dived for them, and missed. They fell to one side of the remaining end rope, leaving the rubber hoses looped around it. He stared down.

The torch had fallen nearly to the full length of the hoses, the bottles only three feet. They hung, clanking together. The torch was swinging, twisting, spurting out flame and level with Cropper's face.

Chris could only stare. Every muscle in his

body seemed to be locked.

The loudhailer came in with inhuman lack of emotion. 'The gas bottles, Chris! Turn off the gas.'

He saw then what Jeff meant. There were valves on the bottles as well as those on the torch. But he couldn't reach them. One armpit was hard over the protective rail, his other fingers reaching for the hoses. He risked a glance beyond the bottles. The tip of the flame brushed Cropper's shoulder, and passed on in its swing. His donkey jacket puffed with flame and smoke for a second. Then he realised he couldn't draw up the hoses, or the torch would fall across Cropper's face.

Chris got up on his knees, suddenly furious, and hammered at the guard rail with the heel of his hand. It came free, and he tossed it away. Now, flat on his chest, his stretched fingers just touched the bottle, then found a valve. He didn't dare look at Cropper. He'd caught a whiff of scorched flesh.

He reached. Pain jolted his shoulder. He gripped the valve feebly between two fingers. It moved. He was screaming to himself: his eyes! He turned the valve a little more. The flame hissed past Cropper's ear.

'You got it,' called the loudhailer. 'Now the

other one. The red one, Chris.'

He stared down dazedly. The flame had become weak and flabby, like a played water hose, but was longer than before, and yellow. His brain didn't seem to be operating.

'The other one, Chris. You must.'

They couldn't lift Cropper past the flame. He groaned, and reached again. The red, the red, he whispered. Smoke was swirling from the flame, blinding him. He touched the cylinder and worked his fingers round it, touched the valve, and eased himself farther forward with his chest and shoulders well over, and found the valve. Frantically he turned it, and at last the flame faltered, and died. He lay panting.

'Good man. We'll pull him up,' the loudhailer said flatly, like a bored station announcement.

Cropper came up slowly towards him. It was impossible for Chris to lift him onto the surface of the chair. They brought him up close, so that Chris could steady his shoulders. Cropper's face was black from the smoke. He'd lost his eyebrows and a lot of his hair.

They were winched in. Many hands reached for Cropper. 'Gently,' Chris croaked, and somebody helped him onto the cliff. The gas bottles clanked on the rock.

They made a carpet of donkey jackets and laid Cropper on them. 'Let me see,' Chris demanded, and crouched over him. Cropper was unconscious, his breath rasping. Chris looked up at Jeff whose face was sallow.

'His ribs . . . and burns . . . ' Chris tried to explain.

There was a crowd round them. Jeff was abruptly very cold and precise, turning on them, police alike, waving his arms and shouting violently. They fell back.

Chris continued to mumble: 'The bar . . . the bar's out of the way now. Mend the chairlift . . . I've got to go back. Let me go back . . . '

'Don't be a fool,' said Jeff.

'Johnny . . . I didn't even get a look. I've got to go back.'

Chris could feel the crowd closing in on Cropper, their gruesome fascination excited by his suffering. He felt disgust choking him. As he turned to face the bridge, it became disgust with himself. Not once had he done enough. Not once had he tried everything possible. He looked out at the creaking bulk of his enemy and accepted that fear had beaten him to the very end. He hated the bridge, and feared it. He began to weep. He wept because he could not get down to it again before he had time to contemplate and reflect on this final failure, and feel it undermine him and any shred of confidence he might have had left.

It was only slowly that he came to the realisation that everything had gone quiet. Jeff and one or two of his men had piled Cropper into a van and taken him as far in the direction of the hospital as the floods would allow. Wearied by the excitement, and persuaded by the men's departure that the action was now taking place elsewhere, most of the public had retired from the scene, followed by many of the policemen. Chris sat on the wet rock, and failed to make himself think.

A shadow moved. Laura approached him. She sat beside him and cried.

'He'll die now, won't he?' she wept.

'Don't cry,' he said thoughtlessly, crying himself. 'He'll be okay.' The words rang hollow, most of all to Chris himself. His words would all ring hollow, and nothing he could say would comfort her. He reached to put his arm round her, and she flinched. She couldn't prevent herself from crying out.

'What is it?' he demanded sharply. 'You're hurt, aren't you?'

'It's just my shoulder.'

'Let me see.'

'No, please . . . '

She moved her hand weakly, but he had pushed her jacket and her clothing to one side and was looking at the bruising on her shoulder. It was purple and green and swollen.

'I fell against an old plough,' she explained.

'What's going on? There's something you're not telling me.'

'You? What should I tell you? *Why* should I tell you? Because you're a doctor? And what good would a doctor do? You can't even look after your own patient. How do you think you'd be able to stop *him*?'

She knew she had said too much. Her face crumpled and her tears coursed down the runnels this produced.

'Stop who?' he said, pushing his sympathy to one side. 'Stop who?'

Laura said nothing.

'You know him, don't you? There is only one him. One man who's done this to you, who's tried to sabotage the rescue. You know him! Who is he? Why's he doing this? You knew him all the while. You know where he is this very minute.'

She remained silent, but it was too late for silence.

'He's tried to kill me, and you know who he is! You knew it was him who burnt the caravan,' he ranted. 'Shot at me and tried to wreck the chairlift. All the time you've known he was trying to kill me.'

She shook her head stubbornly.

'Then what?' he demanded angrily, nearly rising to his feet.

'It was Johnny he was aiming for. Always Johnny. He only got at you because you were his doctor.' She sounded like she was making excuses.

'Oh, that's all right then,' he burst out. 'Nothing personal. You sound like that policeman. He's looking for him, you know. For murder. I know all about him. I'm going to find Grey now, tell him I know his man's identity — '

'No!' she cut in violently.

'Tell me why not.' He was losing his patience, and his head was throbbing as he tried to control himself. 'And tell me why *you* haven't handed him in.'

'I've told you.'

'You haven't told me anything.'

'I have. I've told you what matters to me. My son. Only Den knows where Harry is. Den and Johnny. And Johnny . . . '

Chris refused to accept her reasoning. 'He's insane. A murderer.'

'He's my son.'

She meant Harry. Chris knew that she must have meant Harry. But the way she said it was enough to confuse him. He became distracted slightly by sounds of a new, larger crowd reappearing at the cliff. They had regrouped after the accident. They had taken time to speak to each other, to share the bits of knowledge and the fears they had accumulated since the slings were employed. They had felt the rock shudder; they knew their homes were in danger. Now, with the police cordon weakened, they were pressing forward. He heard some shouts, several manic voices, threatening to cut the bridge.

Chris was still trying to make sense of what was going on — of Laura's words and Cropper's eyes and the revived intentions of the mob — when he felt the first blow to the back of his head. It did not knock him unconscious. His eyes were still open. Laura was staring beyond him with sudden startled horror, and with recognition. The second blow followed so quickly that her look had not changed at all when his head seemed to split open. Then he felt nothing more.

20

Den had been at the bridge for a while. As soon as he had woken, he had climbed back into the Mini and driven most of the way there. He had parked inconspicuously by the side of the road, and walked the remaining distance unseen, gun in hand.

The so-called rescue attempt appeared to him little more than a farce. The man in charge had disappeared, and those he left behind scarcely seemed capable of opening a tin of sweetcorn without getting something wrong. He heard the almighty crack, and knew that it could only bode well for him. He had seen the doctor go out with that moron, and was ready to shoot at them, but soon realised he wouldn't have to. They tried to cut through a hanger bar as though it was nothing more than an elastic band — and of course, it snapped. The rest was pure comedy. It made Den wish that he was the sort of person who could make that sort of thing up. The fat one was dangling like a tired old conker, and the doctor clambering like an idiot chimpanzee. When the torch had cut one of the ropes, that was priceless. And then when it slid off and hung beside that man, setting his hair alight and burning his eyes . . . Den knew that this would be his best chance.

He watched them think of nothing but the injured fool. He watched the crowd disperse — taking the pigs with them — and the men cart their colleague off to the middle of nowhere. And just as he had guessed, no one looked twice at the cutting equipment.

True enough: that doctor sat right beside the torch and the bottles. Sat like a wreck, probably incapable of even smoking a fag. And then . . . that was Laura! What better; a chance to kill two birds with one stone. He had watched them talk for a while. He wouldn't have bothered, but he knew that they were talking about him, and that made him laugh. But after a few minutes he had got bored of being amused and crept up behind the doctor.

Bang! He brought the butt of the gun down onto the back of his head. He paused a moment to smile at Laura, maybe even wink at her. He was keen to show her that she was next. And bang, the doctor was unconscious. Dead, even. Who could say? A doctor, perhaps? Was there a doctor in the house? Well, a conscious one, anyway.

He gave Laura a tap on the head as well.

Not as hard, but then it didn't need to be. He could hear the crowd growing again. He guessed that they were coming to cut the bridge. He always liked to think that others could benefit from actions that served his own ends. He would save them the hassle of having to argue with these nobodies, and save them the effort of having to force their way through.

He went over to Cropper's cutting gear. The doctor had managed to turn the gas off after all, so Den had to dig out a light. He turned the valve and the gas caught at once, spitting out an imprecise orange flame. He turned the other valve and the cone roared blue. Den grinned like a lunatic in the heat, knowing that his work was almost done. He squatted down to Prescott's chains, and the flame dug in.

The chains put up no little resistance. The huge iron links had stood proud for 150 years, and were not about to bow down for the whim of a coarse murderer without some kind of struggle. Den's hands grew hot, and his thoughts turned to the gloves which Cropper must have been wearing on the chairlift. He looked around him, but could see nothing. Cropper must still have been wearing them. He pulled his sleeves down over his hands, losing a little grip, but making the pain more bearable. As the metal began to give way, it spat small splinters of molten steel at Den's face. He had to turn away. This made it harder to concentrate, made it feel like his cutting was less focused, less accurate; but there was no other option. He had thought it would be easy, had imagined a hot knife going through a packet of butter, but it had begun to annoy him now. As he looked away, he willed the bridge to fall. He began to picture Johnny in the truck; the bridge falling, and with it the truck, and with the truck Johnny; the whole mass of metal and concrete and whisky and bone and flesh plummeting into the swollen river; and that made him feel a lot better. As he turned back to his work and saw that most of the foot of metal of his chosen link was reaching its breaking point, he began to feel liberated. It was a freedom he had never felt before. A freedom from the last few years; a licence no longer to have to look over his shoulder; to drink whisky with a smile on his face. Freedom from Laura and the chains which bound him to her; from some son of hers he knew nothing about; from Johnny Parfitt and his mind-numbing stupidity; from Superintendent Grey and his dead son who had deserved everything he got for following blindly in his honest father's honest footsteps, and for driving too fast behind a heavy goods vehicle.

Like Chris, Den had no idea what hit him. Like Chris, the first blow failed to render him unconscious. Den fell onto his back, dropping the torch away from his body. He looked up. A thickset silhouette provided him some brief shelter from the rain. He recognised his assailant. Grey was lifting the gun high above his head, his eyes wild, intent on bringing the butt down onto Den's forehead with as much force as possible. He had no thought in his mind. He wielded the shotgun like an axe, and felt through its muzzle nothing but the potential to end a life. To save his own by ending the life of this animal.

As he looked down at Den, supine, awaiting death, he saw before him the face of his son. Still he did not hesitate. But the first blow had not been true enough. Den did not need him to hesitate. He rolled swiftly to his right and reached for the torch. Grey brought the gun down hard into the ground. He felt the cliff quake beneath him, the pain of the reverberation against his hands, and he dropped the gun.

Den turned to face him, brandishing the flame. He felt no pain. He thought he might even enjoy this. Getting rid of Johnny, of Laura, her meddling doctor and Grey all in one go — not a bad night's work. Grey sidestepped as Den came at him, and gave a wild swing with a fist. As though his fists would do him any good now, Den laughed to himself. He would toy with this policeman, he decided; make him realise just who had been in control all these years. And who, for the last two days, had been in control of everything.

As they stood still, facing each other, knowing that one of them had to die, they heard a huge, slow chugging noise in the background. Den knew better than to turn round, and Grey could see little over his shoulder. The cavalry was arriving. Not on the cliff top, but down below them, in the cutting on the east side. The Jones approached, Marty at the controls, Marson hanging on at the side and howling like a kid playing cowboys. They were oblivious of the tussle going on at the cliff top. The only thing on Marson's mind was the crane's hook and the cab of the truck. Just like he had promised all those hours ago, he was going to pick that truck right off that bridge.

Tony, in the Kato on the west side, looked on in amazement. He could sense the new surges in the crowd's discontentment. He had seen what had happened to Cropper, and had known that there was nothing he could do to help. He had caught sight of the bright flashes

237

of light over by the main support chains on the east side, and though he could not believe it, he knew that someone was trying to cut the bridge. There was no time to disentangle the Kato, so he had given as much line as possible, and had jumped ship. And now, as he looked down to the opposite cutting, he could see the Jones. The Jones, for which they had waited almost two whole days. The Jones, the answer to everything, the culmination of the entire operation. The Jones was here to save the day. And as he watched the manic waves of the torch over on the east cliff top, he knew that it had come too late to save anything. He ran as far from the cliff top as he could, running west for his life.

Den was still fencing with Grey. Grey had no weapon, and he had his back to the cliff, but still Den was reluctant to go for the kill. He even had time for words.

'I hear you've been looking for me,' he said.

Grey did not give him the satisfaction of a reply.

'Haven't you? Four long years, chasing my tail. Well, here I am, Superintendent. You've found me. Or rather, I found you. Aren't you going to get me? Or are you going to die as well? Another useless piece of filth. Can't do his job without being killed. You know what they say, don't you? Like father, like — '

Laura ran at him like she had never run at him before. She slammed her fists into his back and kept on running. The torch flew from his hands over the edge of the cliff. The red and black gas bottles followed quickly behind, plunging down into the churning river below. As Laura looked to see what she had done, Grey turned to look with her. Den had disappeared. They stepped closer to the edge, and they heard his shouts.

'Help me! Help me, Laura, please!'

He was holding on to the chain, Prescott's chain, the very chain he had been trying to cut. The rusty metal bit into his palms and his knuckles were pure white. His legs swung from side to side beneath him as he tried to clamber up and get more of a hold. But he was too heavy. He looked like a monkey.

'Please, Laura! Superintendent! Please!'

'Where's Harry?' demanded Laura. Her voice was cold. She felt that, for the first time, she saw Den for exactly what he was. A worthless, self-serving, cold-blooded bully, as happy to kill as to cry.

'Harry?' screamed Den. 'I'll tell you, Laura. I'll tell you if you help me up.'

'I won't ask you again,' she said. 'Where's Harry?'

Den felt his world collapsing beneath him. 'I don't know,' he called out. One of his hands slipped from the chain. 'Honestly. I don't know.'

'Then what good are you to anyone?' said Laura, turning away.

Den reached up with his free hand, trying to get a hold on the chain again. He succeeded, grasping at it and pulling himself up with all his strength.

The Jones had gone as far as it could go into the narrow roadway. From that distance, it was able, just, to lift the cab and its trailer. Under Marson's direction, Marty was trying to thread the hook into the broken driver's window, to support the cab and its load from the angle between the door and the windscreen. It was taking several attempts. The hook had already smashed the windscreen itself, showering the injured driver with chunks of broken glass. Marson was now shouting instructions as relentlessly as a boxer's trainer shouts into the ring from his corner. Marty was trying to thread the eye of a needle. He had it. No, not quite. The hook swung again. Yes, he had it, Mr Marson, he had it.

Den's strength was too much. A chain is only as strong as its weakest link, thought Grey. And in Prescott's chain, one link was now considerably weaker than all the others. Den's grip and tug finished the job he had not had time to complete with the torch. The chain snapped, and with it snapped its partner. Den was forced to let go, and he plummeted, somersaulting once slowly in the air and then falling head first towards the river. Above him, the bridge dropped and the truck lurched. The platform swung down, hanger bars smashing around it on either side like slithers of broken glass.

On the west side, the crack finally gave way. Hundreds of tons of argillaceous rock broke free from the cliff and dropped into the river as though it had never been attached. The truck began to drop. The line on the Kato began to uncoil itself like a snake stabbed into action.

'I've got it, Mr Marson!' cried Marty. And all at once, neither of them knew what was happening.

The trailer and the cab began to fall into the river. It seemed like it was falling for an eternity, but it had no time to pick up speed. In an instant the line from the Kato twanged solid. A fraction of a second later, the line from the Jones did the same. The old hydraulic crane shook, sending Marty's head into the controls, and Marson's body flying into the side of the cutting. The bridge and the west cliff continued to fall. It shot down towards the river, towards the spot in the churning distance where Den had disappeared.

The bridge, chains, bars, platform and all, hurtled down and crashed into the surface. The white froth it created sprayed almost as high as the cliffs themselves. The crowd watched and waited. No one dared breathe. They listened intently to the sound of the river as it accepted its new gift. The cliff on the east side had stayed intact — only the chain had broken. And so there were hundreds — not thousands — of tons of rock and metal in the river. Slowly, the load began to sink, and the froth began to die down. The crashing eased, and the water appeared to begin to flow around its new obstacle. The level of the river on either side changed little, and soon settled back to its steady rush.

And in mid-air, lower than the level of the roadway and the bridge which had now disappeared altogether, hung an object little short of a miracle. With a thin line stretching from each cliff, one from the cliff top, the other from a cutaway, a forty-ton truck was suspended high above the river. It looked like a toy; a dinky car, flying magically with the aid of a child's hand. Between them, the Kato and the Jones had somehow coped with the dual jerk of the tightening cables, with the brief acceleration of the load under gravity. A wagon-load of whisky hung almost motionless in the air, halfway between the two cliffs.

The only sound over the flow of the river came from Marson's Land-rover. A voice crackled, desperate and confused: 'Laura? Laura?'

Laura ran over to the doctor, crying with joy. 'He's alive!'

Chris sat up, rubbing the back of his head. He put his arm round her. Down in the cutaway, Marson picked himself up. He paused for a moment, then began to calculate the best way to bring him in.

THE END

STRANGER IN THE PLACE

Anne Doughty

Elizabeth Stewart, a Belfast student and only daughter of hardline Protestant parents, sets out on a study visit to the remote west coast of Ireland. Delighted as she is by the beauty of her new surroundings and the small community which welcomes her, she soon discovers she has more to learn than the details of the old country way of life. She comes to reappraise so much that is slighted and dismissed by her family — not least in regard to herself. But it is her relationship with a much older, Catholic man, Patrick Delargy, which compels her to decide what kind of life she really wants.

SECRET OF WERE

Susan Clitheroe

Blessed with wealth and beauty, Miss Sylvestra Harvey makes her debut in the spring of 1812, and she seems destined to take London society by storm. Sylvestra, however, has other ideas; she is set upon marrying her childhood friend, Perry Maynard. What better way, then, to cool the ardour of her admirers than to nurture rumours of a scandalous liaison between herself and the dangerous Marquis of Derwent? This daring plan is to lead Sylvestra into mortal danger before she finally discovers the secrets of her own heart.

ONE BRIGHT CHILD

Patricia Cumper

1936: Leaving behind her favourite perch in the family mango tree in Kingston, Jamaica, little Gloria Carter is sent to a girls' school in England, to receive the finest education money can buy. Gloria discovers two things — one, that in mainly white England she will always need to be twice as good as everyone else in order to be considered half as good; and two, that her ambition is to become a barrister and right the wrongs of her own people. Ahead lies struggle — and joy. The road stretches to Cambridge University, to academic triumph and a controversial mixed marriage. Based on a real-life story.

PROUD HEART, FAIR LADY

Elayn Duffy

Viscount Philip Devlin is not a happy man. From his grave, his father has decreed that the Viscount shall marry a girl he has never met if he is to inherit his beloved Meadowsdene and Kingsgrey Court. For a girl with no dowry to speak of, marrying into one of the oldest, richest houses in England is good fortune indeed. But the Viscount's bride, Kathryn Hastings, faces a grim future for she will be his wife in name only, leaving him to pursue his life as before. Kathryn decides to enact her revenge and turns the tables on Devlin.

DUMMY HAND

Susan Moody

When Cassie Swann is knocked off her bike on a quiet country road, the driver leaves her unconscious and bleeding at the roadside. A man later walks into a police station and confesses, and they gratefully close the case. But something about this guilt-induced confession doesn't smell right, and Cassie's relentless suitor Charlie Quartermain cannot resist doing a little detective work. When a young student at Oxford is found brutally murdered, Charlie begins to suspect that the two incidents are somehow connected. Can he save Cassie from another 'accident' — this time a fatal one?

SHOT IN THE DARK

Annie Ross

When an elderly nun is raped and murdered at a drop-in centre for drug addicts, the police decide it's a burglary gone wrong. Television director Bel Carson sees pictures of the body, and is convinced that this was a ritualistic murder, carried out by a sadistic and calculating killer. Then he strikes closer to home, and Bel determines to track him down. As she closes in on the monster, she senses that someone is spying on her home. And, in a final, terrifying twist, she finds herself caught in the killer's trap . . .